HELLO GOODBYE

HART'S RIDGE

KAY BRATT

BOOKS BY KAY BRATT

HELLO GOODBYE

A Hart's Ridge Novel

Printed in the United States of America

First Printing, 2023

ISBN 979-8987966846

Red Thread Publishing Group

Hartwell, GA 30643

www.kaybratt.com

Cover Design by Elizabeth Mackey Graphic Design

This book is a fictional dramatization that includes one incident inspired by a real event. Facts to support that incident were drawn from a variety of sources, including published materials and interviews, then altered to fit into the fictional story. Otherwise, this book contains fictionalized scenes, composite and representative characters and dialogue, and time compression, all modified for dramatic and narrative purposes. The views and opinions expressed in the book are those of the fictional characters only and do not necessarily reflect or represent the views and opinions held by individuals on which any of the characters are based.

CHAPTER 1

Taylor Gray always thought of nature as a gift for the soul and, as she drove through the winding roads, her eyes were drawn to the breathtaking beauty that surrounded her. Tall, majestic pine trees adorned the landscape, their emerald-green branches reaching up to touch the cerulean sky. Sunlight streamed through the leaves, creating intricate patterns of light and shadow as she drove past. Her window was down, and the air was crisp and fragrant, carrying with it the earthy scent of pine needles and the faint aroma of wildflowers.

She'd never get tired of the beauty of her county. Around Hart's Ridge, it was as if the very essence of nature had painted a masterpiece in every direction. The Blue Ridge Mountains loomed in the distance, their rugged peaks cloaked in a tapestry of deep greens and rich browns, a testament to the timeless power of the earth.

Her phone buzzed, momentarily interrupting this moment of serene contemplation. With a sigh, she reluctantly tore her gaze away from the scenic wonderland that surrounded her.

It was from the sheriff. An address and a message to get there.

Stat!

Tuesday nights were often uneventful, but the sheriff's terse communication hinted at another somber task ahead.

A long time ago, she used to believe that bad things happened to remind her to remember what good was supposed to look like but, lately, as crime seemed to tighten its grip on her beloved Hart's Ridge, she couldn't help but question that belief. The town, once a haven of tranquility, now felt besieged by a relentless wave of misfortune, and she couldn't shake the unsettling feeling that some malevolent force had taken hold.

Though her thoughts were entangled with the weight of recent events and the lingering sorrow from the abrupt end of her blissful high following Sam's proposal, Taylor knew she had no time for introspection now. The sheriff's urgent directive demanded her immediate attention, and she accelerated down the winding road, leaving behind the breathtaking beauty of the Georgia mountains, if only for a moment.

She also didn't have time to dwell on Sam, the subject that had occupied her mind endlessly all morning. She was still sad that the blissful high from his proposal a few weeks ago had only lasted for what felt like minutes before one phone call had brought it to a screeching halt.

Sam has a daughter.

A twelve-year-old daughter named Alice.

Taylor hadn't seen her yet, but she could just imagine a perfectly proportioned little girl with blonde hair, a headband, and bright blue—innocent—eyes.

Sam's eyes.

Mind blown.

All the time they'd been dating, she thought she was the only one who led a trail of family dysfunction and carried baggage into the relationship. She'd thought Sam was squeaky clean.

Completely Beaver Cleaver and All-American Boy. No record, crazy ex-wives, and definitely no children.

Turns out that everyone has a skeleton in the closet. Some just hid theirs better.

She arrived at the scene and parked on Mount Pleasant Street in front of the Swanson's home. There were already ribbons and barricades up, and she saw the sheriff's truck as well as several other county units. An ambulance was there, but the lights were off.

Not a good sign.

Taylor had been there before, just a few weeks prior when there was an altercation between the eldest son and his parents after he'd missed curfew. She'd met two brothers sitting on the lawn, then one had ended up staying overnight with Taylor's dad.

She turned off her car as she tried to think of their names.

Larson.

Oh, and his brother, Marc.

They'd looked like clean cut, respectful teenagers. Not the usual rebellious thugs she usually dealt with around town. She remembered feeling irritated at the parents for being so upset over barely missing a curfew that they wouldn't allow their son to come in.

Ridiculous.

She got out of her car and recalled that the brothers, and their little sister, were adopted. Not recently, either. The little girl was adopted from South Korea, but Taylor hadn't met her. Abby, they'd called her.

Taylor winced. Death was in the air, and she smelled it all around her.

She approached Deputy Grimes, who was stationed at the perimeter. He didn't say anything, only shook his head solemnly.

"It's bad, isn't it?" Taylor asked.

He nodded.

Grimes was a good cop, but he had teenage daughters. If

something had happened to the kids here, he was going to need some time to process it. It was always hard to separate work from family life when similarities crossed in these cases.

Taylor patted him on the back comfortingly, and he looked away.

Shane came out of the house with the sheriff, both of their faces set as grim as Taylor had ever seen them. The call out had barely told anything, so she was going in blind.

"What's going on?" she asked as they approached.

"Double murder," Sheriff said, shaking his head.

Taylor felt sucker-punched and instantly saw the faces of the boys in her mind.

"They have three kids. Please tell me it wasn't them," she said.

"It's the parents," Shane said, his voice somber. "And it's brutal. Especially the mom."

A mobile crime lab drove up, screeching to a stop. Sheriff had obviously called it in.

"Tell me everything," Taylor said.

"Kimberly Swanson, age fifty-one and mother of three, found deceased in the back yard. Appears to have been sexually attacked on top of being bludgeoned to death," Shane said.

"Bishop Swanson, age fifty-three and father of the three, found stabbed to death inside. There was some sort of chase through the house, and he put up a fight. Hands are covered in defensive wounds," Sheriff added. "The two kids at home ran to their house this morning in a panic."

"Which two?" Taylor asked.

"Teen boy and little girl," Shane said.

"I bet I know which son is missing," Taylor said. "I was called out here several weeks ago when the parents refused to let the oldest son in because he'd missed curfew. There was a lot of tension brewing between him and his father. What are you thinking?"

"Not that," Shane said. "That one is out of town doing time at a behavioral health facility. This looks like a home invasion, and the two surviving kids were upstairs sleeping. The little girl came into her brother's room crying in the middle of the night, saying she thought she saw someone outside her window, but he assumed she was having a nightmare. He settled her down and they slept until morning."

"Oh my God," Taylor said. "That's horrible. Did she see the attacks?"

"No, only saw her mother's body on the ground but it looked like a gray figure to her."

Poor Abby. She'd grow up wondering if she had only been successful in alerting her brother that something was going on she could have saved their mother. Taylor's heart already hurt for the little girl who would become a guilt-ridden young woman.

"Can I do a walk through?"

Sheriff nodded. "Shane, take her. I've got to make some calls."

Shane led Taylor into the house, their footsteps echoing in the eerie silence. The air was thick with tension as they followed the trail of blood, a morbid path that told a story of violence and struggle.

They went down to the basement and came to the first body. Shane knelt, examining the defensive wounds on Bishop Swanson's hands. "He put up a fight, that's for sure."

Taylor's eyes scanned the room, taking in the signs of struggle. "There was a chase through the house. Furniture overturned; blood smeared all over the floor. It's like he was trying to protect his family."

"Look at that," Shane said, pointing to an upturned end table. Next to the end table was a big recliner facing a television, a pool of blood beside it.

Taylor nodded, her eyes scanning the room. "The whole place has been torn apart. They could've been searching for something."

They moved from room to room, each one bearing the scars

of a desperate invasion. Taylor couldn't help but shiver as they came across a bloody palm print on the glass door leading to the backyard.

"The perp left in a hurry," Shane commented, studying the print.

"Yeah, maybe they were interrupted," Taylor replied, her mind racing with possibilities. "Or it could be from one of the victims."

Heading outside, the scene was no less gruesome. Kim Swanson's body lay in the yard, a shocking contrast to the peaceful, suburban setting. She was on her back and her legs were splayed open, her arms over her head.

"Oh my God," Taylor muttered, her hand instinctively going to her mouth and almost dropping the notepad she'd pulled from her pocket.

Shane's face was grim as he surveyed the scene. "Correction. Bludgeoned and stabbed. Then sexually assaulted. This is brutal. We have the murder weapon for the head injury. It's a maul they used to cut firewood. It's already logged for evidence."

"I hope we can get some prints from it," Taylor said.

They walked closer to the body, careful not to disturb the crime scene. Taylor's eyes were drawn to the woman's lifeless form, her thoughts filled with a mix of sorrow and anger.

"Why would someone do this?" Taylor wondered aloud.

Shane shook his head, his expression troubled. "We'll have to piece it together. But right now, we need to talk to the kids."

"No blood on her palms," Taylor said, making a note on her pad.

When they came back around to the front of the house, a truck was just pulling up. A man got out and strode up to the deputy who was guarding the perimeter.

"I can't believe it," Taylor said.

"How the hell did he know what was going on?" Shane said under his breath. "He's got a lot of balls to show up here."

They watched as the sheriff joined the deputy and Clint

McElroy at the police tape ribbon, their heads down as they conferred.

Taylor felt a bit shaky at the sight of Clint. He'd been fired from the department at least two years before, and he'd made it clear that he blamed her. He'd always resented her, even before he'd lost his job. He was the kind of man who thought women should be barefoot and pregnant, serving sandwiches and lemonade on the porch. The fact that he and Bishop were close gave her a bit of a window into what kind of man lay dead in the house.

Finally, Clint stomped back to his truck, his face red with anger, and the sheriff came to them. He gestured toward the street where Clint's taillights were receding.

"I told him he can't be here. He's a friend of Bishop Swanson's," Sheriff said. "Said they go to church and play golf together. The neighbor called him."

"Damn it," Shane said. "He was told not to give out any information whatsoever."

"Better go talk to him," Sheriff said. "He's got all the inside right now because of those kids. I don't want this investigation compromised."

Taylor followed Shane across the lawn and up to the house next door. An elderly man opened and showed them in. He was deathly pale.

"Name?" Shane asked.

"Donald. Donald Logano. I just can't believe this," he said, his hand shaking as he held it out to them. "Bishop and Kim are—I mean were—such good people. This is a loss of gigantic proportion. To our neighborhood. Our church, and those kids."

"Yes, Mr. Logano. We understand how this could shake you up. Did you know them long?" Taylor asked, hoping to get a bit of information before Shane lit into him for calling McElroy.

He nodded. "We became good friends just as soon as they moved into the neighborhood five years ago. Bishop had retired and has been a great lookout for everyone else who works all day. Kim is a beloved teacher at the high school. They both hold positions in our church. Always giving, straight from the heart. I just can't imagine who would do such a thing. And my wife is terrified, I'll tell you. She wants to go stay with her mother until you find out who did this and get them off the street."

He finally stopped babbling and Shane asked him where the kids were.

"They're in there," he said, pointing at the living room.

"Before we go in," Shane said, "I have something to ask you. Clint McElroy showed up over at the scene, raging like a bull in a China shop. He said he was informed of the incident by you. Is that correct?"

"I ... uh ... well, they're good friends. He and Bishop," Logano said. "I'm sorry. I shouldn't have called him."

"Exactly," Shane said. "That could be considered impeding an investigation. I'd appreciate it if you don't speak of the case, especially since you know more details than anyone else, because of the kids being here."

Logano nodded emphatically. "Yes. Yes, of course. My apologies."

He guided them into the room where the surviving children were being comforted by his wife. She sat in an armchair facing the couch where Larson and Abby huddled together. "This is Susan, my wife," he said, gesturing at her and then the kids. "And that's Larson and Abby."

Larson, the older brother, looked shell-shocked, his eyes red from crying. Abby clung to him, her small frame shaking with fear.

"Hey there," Taylor said gently. "I'm Taylor, and this is Shane. We're here to understand what happened. Is it okay if we ask you some questions?"

Larson nodded, his voice shaky. "Yeah, of course."

Abby remained silent, her dark eyes wide with trauma. Taylor exchanged a glance with Shane before speaking softly to the little girl.

"It's okay, Abby. We just want to hear what you saw or heard last night. Can you tell us?"

Abby glanced at her brother for reassurance before nodding slightly. "I woke up 'cause I heard Daddy scream. I looked out my window and saw a man outside with a shovel on his shoulder."

Taylor exchanged a puzzled look with Shane. "You saw a man with a shovel? Can you describe him?"

Abby shook her head, tears welling up in her eyes. "It was dark. He looked scary."

Larson tightened his grip on his sister. "Abby, remember what we talked about? It might have been a bad dream."

Abby sniffled, wiping her eyes with her sleeve. "But I saw him, Larson."

Taylor's heart ached for the little girl. "It's okay, Abby. We'll figure this out. Thank you for telling us. Is your room upstairs?"

"All the bedrooms are upstairs," Larson said, nodding.

Shane turned his attention to Larson. "And what about you, Larson? Can you tell us what you remember from last night?"

Larson took a deep breath, his voice shaky. "I went to bed around 9 o'clock. My parents were watching TV. I was on my phone watching videos until I got sleepy, then I drifted off. Abby came into my room later and woke me up, saying she saw something outside. I told her it was just a nightmare and she stayed with me."

Shane nodded. "And when did you find out about your parents?"

Larson's eyes welled up with tears. "I woke up in the morning and looked out the window. I saw Mom ... outside. I knew something was wrong."

Taylor placed a hand on his shoulder. "I'm so sorry, Larson."

"The neighbor mentioned a brother," Shane said. "Where is he?"

"He's in a residential behavioral center for teens in Jasper," Larson said. "We were texting just before I went to sleep. Oh, God—I haven't told him yet. Should I call him now?"

Larson looked panicked.

"No, please don't do that. I'll find out which facility and go tell him in person. That's not the kind of news anyone should get on the phone. I'd like for you to keep this to yourself for now," Shane said.

"But everyone in the neighborhood already knows," Larson said, looking at the people who sat at the kitchen table, their neighbors.

"Not everyone. We've kept it tight, and no names have been released, so we'll try to beat the news," Taylor said.

Shane straightened up, his expression determined. "Yes, we'll go straight there now. We're going to do everything we can to find out what happened. And listen, both of you are brave for telling us what you saw."

Larson pulled his little sister closer, his arm around her protectively.

"What's going to happen to us?" he asked, the fear in his eyes obvious to all.

"Right now, my friend Wesley will be coming, and he'll figure out something," Taylor said. "Most likely he'll help you talk to relatives who can take you in."

"Okay, but I don't want anyone to separate us," Larson said. "Abby needs me right now."

"I'm sure he'll do his best," Shane said. "But we've got to run now. If you think of anything else, please call the number on this card. An officer will be taking you through the house shortly for you to see if you can notice any items missing."

He handed Larson his card and they left.

As the door shut behind them, Taylor's mind was racing with the pieces of the puzzle. The conflicting accounts from the siblings, the brutality of the attack, and the presence of the shovel-wielding man all added up to a deeply unsettling mystery.

Taylor couldn't get Abby's solemn, dark eyes out of her mind. The poor girl had gone through being relinquished by her biological family, then finally found a permanent home with a loving mom and dad, only to have it ripped out from under her in one vicious night.

Hello and goodbye, almost in one fell swoop.

Taylor knew that she and Shane had a long road ahead, but she was resolved to bring justice to the Swanson family and to find out who had shattered their lives so mercilessly.

CHAPTER 2

The ride to Jasper was filled with conversation about the new case, and Taylor tried not to show how many times she looked at her phone every half a mile. All she knew was that it was hard to follow your heart when it was even more confused than your head.

> Please, Taylor. Call me.

Sam wasn't giving up.

They hadn't seen each other since the night of the proposal, and the call from Alice. He needed time to sort that situation out, though he seemed to think he needed Taylor beside him to do it. She wasn't angry at him. Just confused. Why hadn't he trusted her enough to tell her about Alice? It made her question the validity of their commitment to each other.

What else was he hiding?

He knew all the dirt on her family. Both Lucy and Jo had children out of wedlock, so why Sam felt he had to hide his child was beyond Taylor's comprehension.

"Taylor? Did you hear me?"

"Oh, I'm sorry. What?"

Shane turned to give her a funny look. "I said, what's the number we're looking for?"

"3452 Lincoln Street," she said. "It's called The Robin's Nest."

"What else is on your mind? I don't think you've heard a word I've said for at least ten miles. You sure aren't here with me."

"Nothing."

"I'm getting vibes that it's some serious nothing," Shane said. "Anyway, we're here. I already made a call to the director and she's meeting us."

He turned into the driveway of a white, two-story building with a perfectly manicured area around it. A high fence went from the sides of the building into the back, and—because of the green material woven through the links—nothing behind it was visible.

"Looks like a luxury prison," Shane said.

Taylor agreed. She wondered what something like this was costing the Swansons.

They parked and then made their way to the double doors.

"It's locked," Shane said, then spotted an intercom buzzer and pressed it.

A woman's voice answered, and Shane explained, then held his badge up to the small camera. The door buzzed open, and he held it for Taylor.

At the front desk, they signed in, gave an explanation as to why they were there, then waited in the small conference room they were shown to. It was only a few minutes later when they heard heels clacking up the hall toward them, and a woman in a peach-colored blazer and khaki pants approached them.

"Hi, I'm Judith Maloney, and I'll be helping you talk to Marc. Our director couldn't make it because of something else that came up, but she's informed me of the tragedy that occurred with Marc's parents last night," Judith explained, her demeanor calm and professional.

Shane's perturbed expression revealed the gravity of the situation. He wasn't accustomed to involving outsiders in police matters, especially when it came to breaking such devastating news.

"I'm Detective Shane Weaver and this is Deputy Gray. May I ask what your role is here?" Shane asked, a note of caution in his voice.

Judith paused, pulling out a chair from the table and taking a seat, folding her hands in front of her. "I'm a certified family advocate and work with parents and children. I've got extensive experience working with kids who have attachment issues, trauma, developmental delays, autism, medical issues, and more."

Taylor listened intently. Marc Swanson's case seemed outside the scope of Judith's typical work, and she couldn't help but wonder why she had been assigned to him.

"And you're assigned to Marc Swanson why?" Taylor asked, her curiosity piqued. As far as she knew, Marc didn't fall under any of the categories Judith had mentioned.

"I also work with children who have been through the foster care gauntlet. Some that have been adopted and others who remain in the system. Many of them have ongoing issues because of what they've been through, even if they are placed with loving families."

"What can you tell us about Marc?" Taylor said, trying to get a better understanding of just who he is.

Judith leaned back in her chair and sighed. "Marc is a troubled kid. He was abandoned to state custody when he was an infant and went through six foster homes before the Swansons adopted him at the age of eight. They saw problems immediately, and he's had a lot of struggles."

Taylor glanced at Shane, sensing his growing suspicion.

"What about last night?" Shane asked, his tone growing more intense. "Was everyone accounted for at lights out?"

"Absolutely," Judith replied with conviction. "This is a very secure facility, and there are supervisory walk-throughs at specific intervals through the night. Marc was here. He is not your guy."

Taylor couldn't help but feel Shane's skepticism. "We want to talk to him," Shane insisted.

"Of course," Judith said, nodding. "I just ask that you let me tell him the news about his parents. This is a delicate matter, especially when it comes to an already troubled child."

"That's fine, but we want to be right here when you tell him," Shane asserted.

Judith nodded again. "I understand. To see his reaction. I watch *Law and Order*. Follow me, please."

Taylor suppressed an eye roll and followed the woman. There was something unsettling about this situation, and she couldn't shake the feeling that Marc might hold crucial information. The pieces of the puzzle were starting to come together, and it was becoming increasingly evident that this troubled teenager might play a pivotal role in unraveling the mystery behind the brutal murder of his parents.

"Sounds like if he wasn't in lockdown, he might be a person of interest," Taylor whispered to Shane once Judith pulled far enough ahead of them.

"One hundred percent," Shane agreed. "And I'm curious to see just how stringent their process is at night. I think we're going to be here a while."

The sterile, fluorescent-lit corridors of the juvenile behavioral health treatment center felt imposing as Shane and Taylor followed Judith toward a room where Marc, a troubled 17-year-old, lay on a bed with his ankles crossed and his gaze fixed on a TV mounted on the wall. The movie *Top Gun* was playing, and the face of Tom Cruise filled the screen.

Marc was tall and athletic looking. His youthful face bore the unmistakable marks of a tumultuous life, imprinted with a complex mixture of emotions.

Taylor noticed right away that he had a few small bruises on the side of his neck.

"Marc, these are the officials I was telling you about," Judith said gently as she introduced Detective Weaver and Deputy Gray. "They need to speak with you about something important."

Marc sat up and swung his legs around and off the bed, planting them on the floor as he gazed at them. His eyes, a mix of curiosity and guardedness, shifted from one face to the other. His apprehension was palpable, but it was clear that he had been through this process before and probably thought trouble had found him once again.

"Am I being arrested?" he asked.

"For what would you be arrested?" Shane asked, his voice quiet.

Marc shrugged. "I have no idea. But you're cops and you're standing in my bedroom, so two plus two is usually four."

Judith's expression was sympathetic and she sat down beside Marc and put her arm around his shoulders.

He visibly winced but didn't shake her away.

She took a deep breath. "Marc, I know this is difficult, but there's no easy way to say it. Your parents ... last night, there was an incident at your home. It's with great sadness that I have to inform you that they're no longer with us."

Marc's eyes widened with shock, his breath catching in his throat and his facade of indifference crumbling, revealing a teenager overwhelmed by shock.

"Oh God," he whispered, his voice trembling. "What happened?"

"We aren't sure yet. Possibly a home invasion," Shane said.

"Are Abby and Larson okay? Are they safe?"

Taylor exchanged a glance with Shane, noting the genuine concern in Marc's voice for his younger siblings.

"They're safe," Shane replied, his tone reassuring. "They're with the authorities, and they're being taken care of. Someone has called your aunt to come for them."

Relief washed over Marc's face, but it was short-lived. As the reality of his parents' death sank in, his expression hardened once more. The anger he had harbored for them, the resentment of being sent away, appeared to resurface like a tidal wave.

"Good," Marc said coldly, his gaze fixed on the table. "But my parents, well, I'm not sorry about them."

Taylor and Shane exchanged another look.

Marc's response was harsh, but, under the circumstances, not totally shocking. He'd been through more than most his age, and his relationship with his parents was undoubtedly troubled. He was in a locked facility because of them so it would only make sense he'd carry a lot of anger toward them.

Taylor couldn't imagine how terrible it felt to be sent away from the only real home he'd ever had.

"We understand that this must be difficult for you," she said, her tone gentle. "We're here to help you and your siblings in any way we can. If you have any information that might be relevant to what happened last night, please don't hesitate to share it with us."

Marc's gaze remained fixed on the table, his emotions a turbulent sea beneath the surface. As the detectives waited for his response, Taylor couldn't help but wonder if this troubled teenager held the key to unraveling the mystery behind the brutal murder of his parents, or if he was merely a casualty of the tragic events that had unfolded in his life.

"I guess I should ask how they died," Marc said.

"That's still under investigation," Taylor replied. No need to give the kid any of the gory details yet. His brother would probably call him soon with them anyway.

"Did they suffer?" he asked, his face suddenly impassive and unreadable as he looked from Taylor to Shane.

"Again, we cannot disclose any more information other than

that they are deceased," Shane said. "But we do need to take your phone into custody, if you don't mind."

"Why?" Marc said. "Am I a suspect?"

Judith looked alarmed at the request, but she didn't speak.

"No, you are not. It will just help us to eliminate you from any suspicion right away so we can concentrate on the next person," Shane said.

"We just need to download your data and we'll get it right back to you," Taylor said, her voice gentle. "Then you can talk to your siblings, as soon as they are able."

Marc leapt to his feet, shaking Judith's arm off him.

"No way. You aren't taking my phone. You need a warrant for that. I know my rights."

"Sit down," Shane said, stepping forward with his hand out and looking suddenly very scary.

Marc sat back down.

"Thank you. Now, I can get a warrant, but it would be better if you handed it over voluntarily," Shane said.

"Nope, not doing it," Marc said.

"I think you'll need to talk to the director about that," Judith added quickly. "I can take his phone, but I don't have the authority to give it to you. She'll be back in tomorrow."

"I haven't broken any rules," Marc said. "You have no reason to take my phone."

Judith looked at Shane helplessly. "He's right, I'm afraid."

Taylor could see Shane's quiet look of irritation that he tried to hide as he glared at Marc.

"Fine. I guess I'll have to have you down to the station for questioning," Shane said. "And I'll have that warrant then, too. In the meantime, don't delete anything. Our guys will just pull it all back up, so you'll be wasting your time."

Marc got back in place on his bed, his ankles crossed, and his gaze directed to the wall in front of him. He was a sullen teenager again, but he'd won a battle, and Taylor could see that pleased him. They wouldn't get anything else out of him today. But for the fact that every teenager acted like you were going to dismember them if you asked for their phones, his refusal to comply could make him look a bit suspicious, but she didn't want to jump to conclusions.

"One more thing, Marc," Taylor said.

He looked up, his chin defiant.

"How did you get those bruises on your neck?"

He reached up quickly, covering them with his left hand. "They're hickeys. And no, you can't take photos without a warrant."

Taylor and Shane exchanged a look. The kid knew his rights.

"I'm very sorry for your loss," Taylor said, then they backed toward the door.

"Not my loss," Marc said, crossing his arms over his chest. "I gave up on them when they gave up on me."

CHAPTER 3

*T*aylor put her fork down. She should've canceled her and Cecil's dinner date. She couldn't eat or even pretend to. Not with so much on her mind and the sick feeling in her stomach. Most of it was over the brutal murders and the now precarious fate of the three Swanson kids. But, also, she couldn't stop thinking about Sam, and how, with one phone call, the trajectory of their lives was completely changed.

"Talk to me," Cecil said, putting his fork down, too.

"I'm sure you've heard about the Swanson murders," she said. "Nothing stays quiet in this town for long."

Everyone had turned her way when she came into The Den, like the sight of her in her uniform would give them clues as to what the latest was about the terrible crime in their town. The gossip mills were already churning out a lot of scenarios and people were calling the department incessantly to demand answers.

The sheriff ordered her to go home and get some rest while he worked on a search warrant for Marc's phone, DNA, and photos, but she felt the need for Cecil's quiet counsel first. She wished that she'd at least stopped by the farm and changed her clothes before meeting him. Sometimes her uniform was a huge help and, other times, it worked to hinder her emotional wellbeing. The looks as soon as she came through the door seemed to be telling her to get back out there and do her job, that she didn't have time to be eating.

Cecil nodded somberly. "Yes, I have, and it's a damn shame. I didn't know them that well but, from my brief interactions with Bishop and Kim, they appeared to be good people and great parents. All those kids are adopted, you know."

"I know. It breaks my heart that now their lives are upended once again." She felt the sting of tears and kept her gaze down until they evaporated. She could still see the sad and confused look in Abby's eyes as she clung to her brother.

"This is scary stuff. Every woman in Hart's Ridge is locking herself behind barricaded doors before dark each night. The whole darn community is in an uproar fearing that we have a crazed killer on the loose, chasing an innocent mother through the neighborhood and then brutally attacking her."

"Yeah, that's to be expected," Taylor said. "And, to be honest, we can't tell them any different at this point. Everyone is a suspect, yet we don't have a solid lead yet."

"I'm not going to ask you to divulge anything you shouldn't, I'll just say I'm praying for you to find who did it and find them quick. How are the kids doing?"

"Not good. But their aunt is going to take two of them in. The oldest is in state care right now. Not sure what's going to happen to him when he turns eighteen."

"I heard that, too. Poor kid. All of us go through a little rebellion when we're trying to grow up, but some of us take it too far. I hate that he didn't have time to mend that bridge with his parents before their death. "This is a horrific case, and it's going to take a lot from you, Taylor. You know to expect that. I don't have to tell you."

"Yeah. It's going to be rough."

"Maybe my news will brighten your mood." He smiled.

"I hope so. Whatcha got?"

"Guess who's coming to my meetings now?"

At first, she didn't connect the dots, but the way he was smiling, as though it would really make her happy, she figured it out in the next second.

"My dad?"

He nodded proudly. "Jackson Gray. The one and only. He's been six times in a row. Hasn't spoken yet, but he's listening."

Taylor leaned back and let out a long sigh. "That really is good news, Cecil. I know it's supposed to be confidential, so thank you for telling me. I've been trying to get him back to AA for years, you know."

"I know. And you are probably a big reason he came. Even when he appeared not to be listening, your words sank in there somewhere. You can be proud of yourself."

She felt her cheeks warm. "I don't know about that, but I'm glad he's taking that step. I don't think I can handle any more stress at the moment, so to know that he might really be trying to stay sober is a huge weight off my chest. And who knows, it might be his new lady friend pushing him to do better. I hear he's been seen out and about with yet another one. Once a charmer, always a charmer, I guess."

"True. Might have a little to do with it. Not sure how serious he is about the lady friend. It's very coincidental that he is suddenly interested in romance after Cate finds someone."

"Yeah, maybe." Taylor couldn't tell Cecil that Cate and Ellis were having a rough spot. Cate told her in confidence that his adult kids weren't happy with who he was dating, and it wasn't Taylor's place to tell it. She just hoped that they found a way to work things out. She hated seeing Cate looking so sad again.

Cate and Ellis.

She and Sam.

Why were relationships so damn hard?

Cecil's brow wrinkled, sending craggy lines across his face in a dance of worry. "But I can see you're struggling with something else."

He knew her so well.

"Just that I'm a horrible fiancée," she admitted.

"I really doubt that," Cecil said with a slight smile. "But it's okay to feel a little uncertain now that you've committed to being with someone for the rest of your life. I promise, it gets easier after you're officially married."

"It's not that," she said as she sat back in the booth, feeling the energy drain out of her body, making her slump with fatigue.

"Then what?"

Taylor looked around. Sam's news hadn't yet made the grapevine and she didn't want it to, but no one was paying them any attention. The Den was full tonight, most showing up for Mabel's famous chicken livers. She only made them once a week, and they were legendary, though Taylor wasn't a fan. She'd ordered fried chicken, but so far had only nibbled.

Cecil was a fan, though, and his plate was piled high. He usually ate healthier than that, but Mabel's chicken livers were his guilty pleasure that he indulged in once a month. He always said he walked twice his normal distance the day after to expunge the grease and calories.

"Sam just found out that he has a twelve-year-old daughter," she blurted out, then instantly felt a bit of relief. She hadn't told a single soul so far, and now the words felt less heavy in her head.

Cecil didn't look as surprised as she'd expected. He raised his eyebrows slightly, but picked up his fork and took a bite.

"What do you think about that?" she asked him.

He swallowed, then wiped his mouth before speaking. "Well, without more details, I don't really know. On one hand, finding out you have a child you don't know about could be a huge blessing. But there's the question of why didn't he know? Or did he know and choose not to be involved. Or maybe the mother didn't want him a part of their life. Then you might ask yourself why she didn't want him a part of their child's life. Or perhaps he tried and was pushed away. Basically, without further investigation—which you are very good at, I might say—I don't think I'd form an opinion one way or the other."

He had a point, and now Taylor felt childish. She hadn't given Sam the opportunity to explain more. Now he probably thought she was a kid-hater. Or selfish. Or that she didn't want to marry him.

But did she?

That was another question that lurked in her mind. She loved Sam, that was for sure, without a doubt. However, the idea she had of their future together didn't involve stepchildren or a connection to a baby mama. In her years of law enforcement, she'd seen too many serious altercations involving relationships. Many of them because of divorces, second marriages, or stepchildren.

It was a rocky path to embark on and she knew it more than anyone.

"I guess I've reacted badly," she finally said, feeling ashamed. "I probably hurt Sam, and that's the last thing I wanted to do."

Cecil nodded thoughtfully, his silver hair catching the warm, dim light of the cozy den.

"Taylor," he began gently, setting his fork down, "love is a complex journey, and sometimes it takes unexpected turns. Life rarely unfolds exactly as we plan it, and relationships can be even more unpredictable. I've learned a few things over the years, and one of them is that love isn't just about the good times, but also about how we navigate the challenges that come our way."

Taylor listened intently, her worries slowly being soothed by Cecil's calm voice.

"Sam's situation ... well, that's something neither of you could have foreseen. It's not about whether you're a horrible fiancée or not, it's about how you both handle this thing together. Love isn't just about loving someone when it's easy; it's about supporting each other when things get tough." Cecil leaned in a little closer, his voice carrying the weight of his wisdom. "I know—because of your job—you've seen more than the average person about the rocky paths people can take when it comes to blended families. But remember, Taylor, those paths are often made rockier by resistance and lack of understanding. You and Sam have a chance to choose a different route, one filled with empathy, patience, and communication. It doesn't have to be a bad thing."

Taylor considered Cecil's words, her mind slowly shifting from her initial shock to a more open perspective. She realized that she needed to give Sam the opportunity to explain, to understand his side of the story, and then to make a decision together about their future.

Cecil offered her a reassuring smile. "Taylor, love has a way of surprising us, teaching us, and sometimes making us better people. Embrace the uncertainty and remember that it's not about whether this was part of your plan, but how you both adapt and grow together as you navigate this new chapter in your relationship. It's a good thing that this has come to light now. Perhaps God is testing you both before you tie the knot."

Taylor nodded, a sense of clarity beginning to replace the confusion that had clouded her mind earlier. Cecil's words had given her the strength to face Sam and see where they stood. Maybe even face the challenges ahead with more of an open heart and less judgment.

She looked up at Cecil. "Can you get the bill? I have somewhere I need to be and don't want to waste any more time."

"Of course. I had a feeling you'd say that." He reached across the table and put his warm hand over hers, sending sparks of love up through her fingers and straight to her heart. "Taylor, please, be gentle to yourself. You're doing the best you can. Now, go to him. You got this, girl. I believe in you."

CHAPTER 4

Sam was still scanning through Facebook, going on hour three when he saw headlights shine through the living room. He jumped up from his seat at the table and went to the door, Diesel leading the way with a low growl in his throat.

He peeked out the curtain, and when he saw the county car he threw the door open and stood out on the porch, waves of relief flooding through him. It was crazy but, without Taylor, everything felt dark and depressing. He'd spent his days going through the motion, without one ounce of zest for life.

She got out of the car looking wary, but he didn't even give her a chance to speak before he met her at the steps and threw his arms around her. "Oh my God, I've missed you," he murmured in her ear as he held her tightly. He could feel his heart beating out of his chest to have her so close.

Diesel's tail beat wildly against both their legs, waiting for them to pull apart so he could get some loving from his favorite female.

"I've missed you, too," Taylor said softly, then dropped her arms.

He reluctantly let go and stood back, watching as Diesel just about toppled her over with his exuberance. Taylor went down to one knee and gathered him up in her arms, burying her head in his neck for a moment while she gave him a good scratch.

"Alright, alright. Why does he get more love than I do?" he said, then helped Taylor up and led her inside.

"I can rub you behind the ears, too, if you want," Taylor joked as she took off her work belt and gently lay it on the kitchen counter.

She reached up and pulled the pin or whatever it was holding her hair up and it fell like a dark curtain, framing her face and instantly making her look ten years younger. Sam could swear that she got more beautiful every day, but she'd deny it.

Two weeks of not seeing her had made him just about lose his mind.

"Thank you for finally coming," he said softly.

She nodded, barely perceptibly, and went to the cupboard and got a glass.

"I've got lemonade and orange juice," he said, going to the refrigerator. "Rice crispy bars, too."

"OJ will be good." She handed him the glass. "I'll skip the bars."

Sam took his time putting ice in the cup and then filling it up, hoping to figure out what to say next. Should he mention the latest with Alice? Or not bring it up?

"What's going on with Alice?" Taylor asked, deciding for him. "Have you met her yet?"

He handed her the glass and then went to the living room, patting the couch beside him. Taylor joined him and kicked off her shoes. Diesel dropped down beside the couch, looking happy to have both his humans in one spot.

"Hold on a second," Sam said. "Let me see those feet. I know they're hurting."

It was a good sign that she didn't say no and instead leaned back and put her feet in his lap. He could always win points with a foot rub.

"You're avoiding the subject," Taylor said, then closed her eyes and leaned her head back when he began caressing her arch.

"No, I'm not. There's not much going on yet. I'm still trying to get information about her. And, no, I haven't met her yet. Her mother doesn't know that she found me, and she's scared to tell her."

Taylor opened her eyes instantly.

"Hold on. Is Alice afraid of her mom?"

He shrugged. "Sort of. But I asked her if she's in any danger and she said no. I gotta tell you, Taylor, she doesn't talk like she's twelve years old."

"What do you mean?"

Sam wasn't even sure how to explain it.

"It's not that I've been around a lot of pre-teens, but she seems older when she talks. She's so mature."

Taylor sat up and moved her feet off his lap and onto the floor. "I thought you said you haven't met her?"

"I didn't. She texted me a photo. Do you want to see her?" He practically held his breath, hoping that Taylor would say yes. He needed her to help him with this latest revelation. He had no idea what to do. About any of it.

"Okay. Yes, I want to see her," Taylor finally said after a long hesitation.

Sam picked up his phone from the side table and flipped through until he found the string of messages he and Alice had made. He pulled up the photo and then handed the phone to Taylor.

She took it and stared at it for a moment. Then, without saying a word, she handed his phone back.

"What do you think?" he asked, putting the phone back on the table. He'd already looked at the photo at least a hundred times in the last few days. Analyzing it.

"She looks like you."

He felt lightheaded. That's what he'd thought, too.

"She has your blue eyes and the shape of your face. You also both have the same cowlick at your crown," Taylor said, looking at him. "What did *you* think?"

He nodded. "The same. I guess that answers my next question about getting a DNA test."

Taylor leaned back on the couch and put her feet back into his lap. He began rubbing one of them as though his life depended on it.

"Well, I think you should get a test anyway," she said. "And you're going to have to talk to her mother. Unless you don't want to be a part of your daughter's life."

"I don't know what I want, Taylor. Other than you. I *know* I want you in my life. And Diesel. But I still can't get my head around the fact that I have a daughter I never knew about."

"You know how those things are made, right?" Taylor mumbled from under the arm she had laid over her face.

Sam couldn't tell if she was upset that Alice looked like him, or if she was just exhausted. He didn't even know what kind of case she was working on, and that made him feel disconnected from her in a way he hadn't felt since they'd first met.

"Yes, I do know. But usually, if a guy gets a girl pregnant, the girl will tell him. Brooke and I weren't even a thing. I mean, we had a thing, but it was short and nothing serious. Why she wouldn't just tell me is crazy."

Taylor put her arm down and Sam could see her face again.

"So, tell me about Brooke."

He let out a long, shaky sigh and looked straight ahead.

"I had a really good buddy named Josh and she was his older sister."

"How old were you and how old was she?"

"I was twenty. I think she was like twenty-six and had a long-time boyfriend. But one night they broke up and she was crying her heart out to me, and, well, things just happened."

Taylor sat up again. She looked angry. "Just happened? That

doesn't sound accurate. It sounds to me like she was having a vulnerable moment, and you took advantage of that."

"No, that is not true," Sam said, holding his hands up. "She came after me and was relentless. I didn't want anything to do with her, but she kept on until I couldn't say no. I swear, that's the God's truth."

"You poor thing," Taylor said. "So, she cornered you and your penis fell into her, making a baby who has now lived twelve years without a father. Sam, I'm having a hard time finding sympathy for you in this."

She put her head in her hands, and the sight of her looking so upset broke him.

He scooted closer and put his arms around her. "I'm not saying I'm innocent. I was a kid with raging hormones. But I want you to know there were no feelings between me and Alice's mom. It's not like that. And I'm not trying to run away from my responsibility, either. I'll do the right thing. Once I figure out what that is."

Taylor looked up at him. "How did she find you?"

"She found a letter I'd written to her mom. She searched my name online and narrowed it down by area. But really, I think it was by chance she picked me to call."

"What did it say?"

"What did what say?"

"The letter you wrote to Brooke," Taylor said.

"Oh. Basically that I was sorry but wasn't interested in a relationship with her, and that we shouldn't have slept together. It was dated. I guess Alice put two and two together. I don't know."

"You and Brooke never had anything else? Just one fling and that's all?"

"Yes. Nothing else. As far as I know, she went back to that boyfriend. I haven't asked Alice anything about her mom yet. I didn't stay in touch with Brooke's brother, either. He enlisted, and I never heard from either of them again."

"Until Alice," Taylor said, looking hurt.

Sam paused and tried to see things from her point of view. He realized that, as shook up as he was about a daughter just popping into his life, she was probably the same. She was probably confused, shocked, and all the emotions he was feeling, too. Maybe she even thought there was a chance he and Brooke would get together for Alice's sake.

Something that would never happen.

He reached for her hand and was relieved when she didn't pull it back.

"This doesn't change anything about us, Taylor. I still love you and want to marry you. I'd marry you today! Right this second, even. This situation with Alice doesn't have to come between us. It shouldn't. Please, don't let it."

"I'm trying not to, Sam. Really. I'm trying. I just don't know where to go from here."

"I don't either. But I know I need you to stand with me while I figure it all out. I haven't even told my dad. I don't know what to say, or what to do next. I can tell that Alice is reaching out because she needs something. Or someone. But I haven't figured her out yet, either. I mean, what am I supposed to do, just ask her where she lives and walk up and knock on the door?"

Taylor sighed.

"First you need to get Alice to give you permission to have a conversation with her mom. You really can't do anything with just a few phone calls with a twelve-year-old. And if you don't get permission first, you'll break her trust before you even have it. If I were you, I'd advise her that there's a possibility you aren't her dad. Just so she's not getting in over her head."

"I did tell her that," Sam said. There was that possibility, but he still kept seeing his eyes on her young, innocent face.

"Good. Now you need to tell her that if she wants to explore this further you need to talk to Brooke."

"I'll do that tomorrow," he said, crossing his heart with a boy scout's flair. "Now, can we talk about you and me?"

Taylor looked pensive for a minute longer, than her face relaxed.

"What *about* us?"

"Will you go to the concert with me? The one the Hart's Ridge Humane Society is putting on? Your mom has talked Corbin into being their headliner."

She raised her eyebrows at him. "Hmm. You think he'll be able to do it?"

"I don't know, but I think we need to be there to support him, either way. He's been doing a lot of training with Hank, and I think he's ready to get back to work. At least for small things for now. They're calling it *Paws and Pickin'*, and there's a few more artists lined up, too. Should be fun."

"I'll need to check with Sheriff and make sure I'm not scheduled for duty that night. He may even ask me to do security."

"Please tell him no."

Taylor laughed. "We don't tell the sheriff no. But I'll see what I can do. Do you have some boots to wear? You know you can't show up in sneakers, right? What kind of country boy wears sneakers to an outdoor concert?"

She was teasing him and, if she was teasing him, that meant she still loved him. Sam felt his heart swell with joy and relief.

"Oh, I've got some boots. You'd better believe it. They're all worn in and rugged, too. No shine to be seen."

"Perfect. That's how I like my men, too," she said. "Worn and rugged. Not shiny."

"Oh, yeah? What if I said that about how I like my women? Huh?" He tackled her back against the couch, covering her with his body. Her giggly scream brought Diesel up off the floor instantly.

"It's okay, boy. Just tickling our girl." He stopped though because Diesel's expression was so worrisome.

Taylor sat up and tugged on her uniform shirt, straightening it, and tucking it back into her pants. Even in the starched blue, stiff material, she looked sexy as hell. The best thing about it was that she had no idea.

"One more thing," he said. "I have a meeting set up with Kathie Huff, that genealogist I told you about. It's tomorrow at noon. Can you make it?"

She was instantly somber. Expected, considering the subject. He'd gone from making her laugh uproariously to bringing up the most painful thing in her past.

"I can't. You must not have heard about the case I'm working on. It's a double murder."

"What? Really? Who? Do I know them?" He didn't usually hear much town gossip and, though he'd been on Facebook, it was only to try to find Brooke to see if there were baby pictures of Alice posted. He hadn't found her, and he sure hadn't heard anything about a murder.

"Do you remember the kid Marc that I had to pick up and take to my dad's house when his parents wouldn't let him in for missing curfew?"

"Oh, no, don't tell me it was him," Sam said.

"No. It was his parents. Both of them, and it was brutal."

"Weren't there more kids, too?"

She nodded. "Another brother and a little sister. All the kids are fine. Marc was locked up in a behavioral health facility, so he has an alibi. Not that I think he could do something so heinous, though. Anyway, I'm going to be tied up with that for a while. But if you want to talk to the woman on my behalf, I'm okay with that."

Sam's head spun with the possibilities. If he could be instrumental in helping to uncover who had assaulted Taylor, those would be some major brownie points. Even if it wasn't, he wanted to help her put the incident behind her and, until she had someone to blame, she was never going to let it go.

"Yeah, I'll go," he said. "We can at least get started. She sounded like a nice woman, and I think she can help us. Next question. Are you staying the night with us? Diesel wants to know."

He crossed his fingers and held them up in front of a wide smile. Amusingly, Diesel sat next to him with a silly grin.

Her two boys. She loved them so much.

Taylor picked up a throw pillow and tossed it at Sam, laughing.

"Only if you get back to work on my feet," she said, her tone low and sexy.

Feet, he could do. All night long if he had to, though he hoped that a foot massage would lead to other body parts. As he lifted her legs to swing her around and back in position on the couch, he felt light with giddiness. Suddenly his world had righted itself once again.

CHAPTER 5

*T*he fluorescent lights of the high school hallway buzzed overhead as Taylor and Shane waited to meet with Principal Clayton Davis, the head of the school. The air was thick with tension because Shane had just informed Taylor that he and Lucy had gone on a date.

"And you didn't think you should ask me first?" she said, still steaming.

He chuckled. "Why would I ask you? Lucy is an adult, the last time I checked."

"I thought she was going to start seeing Corbin," Taylor said, knowing it would irritate him. "He's been interested in her ever since Jo turned him down. Much more her type, too."

He shrugged. "I guess the best man wins. I have a great job. A steady salary and benefits. A pension. What does Corbin have other than some old songs that no one remembers and a fear of continuing his career? He'll be slinging hamburgers once all his old royalties dry up."

"That's really mean, Shane. And he's doing better. He's going to be singing at an event soon and it would be nice if you'd be supportive."

"Me? I won't be there. I'll probably be taking Lucy to dinner and a movie that night," he sneered.

"Forget it. I don't want to talk about it anymore," Taylor said. "Just so you know, though, benefits and a pension have never been anything Lucy is interested in. You'd better be bringing more to the table if you want to impress her."

"Thought you didn't want to talk about it anymore?"

She breathed deeply, counting to ten. She did want to talk about it, but not to him. She couldn't wait to ask Lucy why she hadn't said something. She'd promised no more secrets after she'd almost lost her life to her old lover's wife.

"Why are you so bent out of shape about it?" Shane asked. "Could it be I was your fallback in case things don't work out with the All-American Boy?"

"Don't be ridiculous."

Taylor didn't know why it bothered her so much. She could've been with Shane, but she'd chosen Sam, and didn't regret it. But Shane sure did switch his attention to a new woman quickly. Her sister, no less.

It showed her even more that she was right not to get involved with him.

"Anyway, what did you say Bishop Swanson did for a living?" she asked.

"Used to be a computer technician. Worked for NASA way back. Mostly retired now. But we had a caller on the tip line offer up a possible lead. Turns out Bishop has been spending most of his Saturdays for the last six months picketing an abortion clinic in Atlanta. The caller said he was bad about getting in their faces when he tried to persuade the women not to go in. Some of them filed police reports. I have Penner looking into that and he should have the names for us tomorrow."

"Anything else you haven't filled me in on yet?"

"Forensics came back on the maul. Nothing. Wiped clean of prints."

"Damn," Taylor said. "What about the handprint on the door?"

"We got that but it's only a partial. It'll be a miracle if they can salvage it. But at least it's something. Also, a report came in that a neighbor found a blood trail in the woods behind his house. A whole block away from the Swansons. A few footprints and some shoe prints."

"He chased her out of the house and through the woods," Taylor said softly. "How terrifying."

"Right. But he must've caught her and led her back to the yard where she was killed. There weren't any drag marks found anywhere."

The principal appeared, his face etched with sorrow and shock. He extended his hand to the detectives, his grip firm yet trembling.

"Detective Weaver, Deputy Gray," Principal Davis began, his voice filled with grief. "I can't express how shocked and devastated we all are about Kim Swanson's death. She's been a beloved teacher here for years, and her loss is deeply felt by both the staff and the students."

Taylor nodded. "We understand, Principal Davis. We hate to intrude but time is of the essence in cases like these and we're here to gather information that might help us with our investigation."

"I'm not sure what I can add that will help," he said. "Ask me anything."

"Tell us about her," Shane said.

The principal led them down the hallway, his footsteps echoing in the empty corridor. "Kim taught English. She was passionate about her subjects and had a remarkable ability to engage her students. At least a hundred or more gathered last night for a candlelight vigil under her classroom window. We've brought in extra counselors today to assist the students who were particularly close to her. It's been a difficult day for all of us."

As they reached Kimberly's classroom, the door stood open, revealing a space filled with history books, maps, and a whiteboard covered in colorful messages from her students. Her desk was laden with flowers, the combined scent of them nearly choking her.

Taylor took in the surroundings, her eyes scanning a few notes left on the board.

We'll miss you so much.

Heaven earned an angel.

"She must have been a wonderful teacher," Taylor said.

Principal Davis nodded somberly. "She was indeed. Her loss leaves a void that will be hard to fill."

Shane picked up the conversation. "Can you tell us who her closest teacher friends were?"

"I'll do better than that. Wait right here." He stepped out of the room briefly and returned with a woman who appeared equally somber.

"Tina teaches history across the hall. She and Kim took all their breaks together and were probably the closest on the staff. Tina, these are the county officials working on Kimberly's case," Principal Davis introduced them. "They have some questions, and I'll be back in my office if you need me."

He left them all standing in the hall outside of Kimberly's classroom.

Tina greeted them with a solemn nod. "Of course. I'll do anything to help."

"Let's go back in here," Shane said. "For more privacy."

They all went in and took a desk in the back corner of the room, away from the door and any prying eyes. Shane flipped open his notebook and took a pen out, ready for notes.

Taylor began her line of inquiry as she and Shane had planned on the way over. "Tina, how long have you known Kimberly?"

"I guess about four years. We got close as soon as they moved here and she started this job. I invited them to join my church and they did, so we saw each other outside of school, too. I'd say we were probably best friends."

Shane jotted down a note then looked up. "We understand that Kimberly was a devoted wife. But given the nature of our investigation, we need to explore all possible angles. Did she ever mention having a romantic interest here at the school?"

Tina's eyes widened in mortification; her voice filled with disbelief. "Oh, no, Detective. Kim was a good, Christian woman, devoted to her husband and her faith. She would never stray from her commitment to either. She was very involved with the church, too. Has been for years."

Taylor couldn't help but appreciate Tina's loyalty to her colleague, but her years in law enforcement had taught her that appearances could be deceiving.

"We appreciate your honesty, Tina," Taylor said, her tone gentle. "But, sometimes, things are more complex than they appear. If you know anything at all that can help, any little thing she told you in confidence, we need to hear it. Murders can happen when secrets are involved."

"No. There was nothing like that," Tina said. "She would've told me."

"If you told each other everything, that means you vented to one another, too. What kind of things did she vent about? Her husband, possibly? I'm sure he wasn't always perfect," Shane asked.

"Kim is the kind of woman who, even if she had issues in her marriage she'd never tell anyone because she was loyal to a fault. We're Catholic and the church teaches us not to ever speak against our husbands."

"They couldn't have children?" Taylor asked.

"I don't know about if they could or not, but I know they adopted those kids because they wanted to help children who had had troubled childhoods. They ran marriage encounter sessions at our church," Tina said. "They'd be the last couple to have marital problems."

"Or admit to them," Shane said, earning him a scowl from Tina.

"Then what did she talk about?" Taylor asked.

"Well, she's got two teenage boys, so you can imagine what most of her venting was," Tina said. "You know about Marc being taken out of the home, right?"

"Yes, and we visited him at the facility," Taylor said.

Tina shook her head sadly. "He's got a lot of problems. Kim used to tell me about some of the things he got into. Bishop had his hands full trying to put Marc on the straight and narrow."

"What are some big things you remember her saying?" Shane asked.

Tina paused, her finger to her mouth. "Oh. I remember that Bishop was very creative when it came to punishments for the boys. Things like painting the shed or cleaning the gutters. One time Bishop made the oldest boy stay outside all night, chopping wood. We had storms that night. Lightening and everything. I told Kim that was too much, but she supported anything that Bishop said. He was the authority under that roof."

Chopping wood. That would've been done with the maul.

Taylor wondered if there was a connection.

"What about Larson? Was he following in Marc's footsteps regarding rebellion?" Shane asked.

Tina shook her head. "No. That I know of, Larson has always been a good kid. Star student, popular with the other kids, and excels in soccer. Kim was so proud of him. For a while they'd planned to send him to seminary after high school, but I don't think that was ever confirmed. Larson is a gentle soul. He has a strong bond with Abby, but he's close to Marc, too. Kim told me

Larson had tried his best to talk them into letting Marc come home. They both came from terrible foster care experiences, and I think that's why they bonded so much."

"What do you know of their childhood?" Shane asked.

"I know that Larson was adopted first when he was about seven after being in the foster system since the age of two. Then Marc came six months later. I forget which one, but one of the boys was the only child of a prostitute and her pimp. I think Kim said that Larson had to scrape food from dumpsters to eat before he was found, so maybe it was him."

Taylor felt sick thinking about what sort of lives the boys must've led when they were barely more than babies. A two-year-old digging for scraps? The cruelness some people could show on children never ceased to amaze her. The world was full of psychos.

"We'd like to see inside Larson's locker," Shane said.

"We'll need the principal for that," Tina said. "I'll take you to the locker, then I'll go get him. Follow me."

Shane closed his notebook and tucked it under his arm. They trailed behind Tina. On the way out of the room, Taylor took one more look at the emotional messages scrawled across the board before she shut the door.

As they continued down the hallway, passing classrooms and students absorbed in their studies, Taylor couldn't help but pause at a few doors with male teachers at the front of the room. Affairs were often at the root of such tragedies. Sometimes even best friends weren't in the loop.

Tina led them to a locker, then left them while she went for Principal Davis.

"What do you think?" Shane asked Taylor.

Taylor shrugged. "She's not really giving us much, though I think she believes that Kimberly would never have a relationship outside of her marriage. She's probably right."

Shane raised his eyebrows. "Ready to give up on that theory *already?*"

"Sure am. Unless you know something I don't."

Principal Davis arrived with Tina and promptly opened the locker for the detectives.

The metal door revealed a typical high school student's life – textbooks, notebooks, a couple of football posters, and a neatly folded letter from a college scout.

Taylor and Shane carefully examined the contents, looking for any clues or items out of the ordinary, but nothing stood out.

As they closed the locker, Tina leaned in close to Taylor and whispered. "Can I ask a question? Is it true that Kim was found in the backyard, her throat slashed, head bashed in, and nude other than one sock?"

CHAPTER 6

*S*am's nerves were up since that morning when he'd texted Alice and told her to have her mom call him, but when he pulled up to the small, brown house out on 412 he instantly felt a sense of warmth from the place. Just a humble home with handmade, wooden shutters, set back off the highway, but it obviously had a loving touch tending to it. There was a fence that surrounded the side and back of the property and he could see a few horses grazing. He shut off the car, grabbed his binder, then followed a pathway of pebbles lined with natural rock and bright red zinnias up to the porch.

A dozen or so hummingbirds fluttered around a few feeders in the backyard.

Across the way, a horse and a donkey came to the fence, curious to see who was visiting. The donkey stuck his tongue out at Sam, making him chuckle.

"Oh, that's Eeyore," a voice said. "He's a clown. The horse is Miss Junebug, and she likes to mess with him, see if she can make him mad. Spoiler alert. She can."

Sam turned to see a petite, dark-haired woman holding the door open. A short-legged, one-eyed rotund dog came racing out and stood between them, his expression fierce as he growled a warning.

She pointed her finger at the dog. "Kaiser, no. He's okay."

He stood down, but he glared at Sam as though daring him to hurt his mistress.

"You must be Kathie." Sam held his hand out, taking care not to step too close. The dog might only have one eye, but he looked like he could give a nasty bite if he felt the need.

She took it and gave him a firm handshake. One touch and Sam could tell this was a woman who knew how to put a good day's work in.

"Come on in. We'll sit out here on the screened porch and enjoy this balmy weather."

He followed her in. The porch was clean and quaint, a blend of rustic finishes with colorful, quilted throws lying over the back of a small couch against the wall. A standing shelf was in the corner, and it was laden heavy with jars filled with pickles, okra, and other canned goodies.

Kathie led him to a small table holding two cups of steaming coffee and a plate of cookies.

"Cream or sugar?" Kathie asked, hesitating before she sat.

"No, thank you."

"Good. You like your coffee like I do. Coffee is serious business. I don't get into all the Starbucks stuff. All the tall, grandes, and soy this or almond that. I go in with my granddaughter and I don't even know what language they're speaking," she said, then sat down and took a long drink.

Sam laughed.

Kathie seemed like a real salt of the earth, no nonsense kind of woman. Perfect for her line of work, actually. Probably meant she was analytical and precise.

"Kaiser, sit." She pointed to the spot at her feet and the dog, planting his chubby butt right at the top of her shoes.

"Those are white chocolate chips and pecans," she said. "Help yourself."

"Thank you." He plucked one from the plate and took a bite, almost groaning with pleasure at the warm burst of flavor that exploded in his mouth. "These are so good," he mumbled, his mouth full.

"They are, aren't they? Jim, my husband, loves them when he gets home from a rough day at the ranch where he's a manager. Comfort food, for sure."

"Ranch manager, huh? That sounds exciting." He pictured a man galloping around on a horse, wearing a Stetson cowboy hat and spurs.

She chuckled. "It can be. Just ask ol' Kaiser here. He gets to go sometimes. Loves to help herd the animals but gets himself in a heap of trouble now and then. He pouts when he has to stay home. Thinks he's Jim's little partner, I think."

Sam looked down at Kaiser, seeing him in a new light. His stubby tail wagged furiously at Kathie saying his name. He really was an intelligent-looking dog, though Sam couldn't imagine his breed doing much farm work or doing it successfully. He looked like some sort of Yorkie mix, but he still carried himself as though he were a Doberman or some other big breed. He had a look in his one eye, too. Like he was challenging Sam to think he was less than capable of anything he wanted to do.

"He's cute," Sam said. "In a gruff kinda way."

Kathie held her finger to her lips. "Shh. Don't tell him he's cute. That will hurt his ego. He thinks he's a rough and tumble cowboy."

They both laughed.

"Speaking of cowboys, I heard your husband is a champion roper. That's a cool hobby," Sam said.

She beamed proudly. "More than a hobby. He's made some good money doing it. Of course, Jim is passionate about it, too. Makes it easier to be a champion when you love doing it so much. I could brag on him all day, but I guess we should get down to brass tacks. How did you find me?"

"Online. I wanted to ask; how long have you been doing this?"

"Oh, a long time," she said, then began telling him her credentials as a genealogy expert, touching on some of the cases she's helped solve. "I wasn't college trained on it, mind you. Learned it all through trial, error, and an everlasting dose of stubbornness. When I get on the trail of a mystery, I don't stop. If I want answers, I will find them. One way or another."

Sam had felt nervous coming without Taylor, but she'd given her blessing and he wanted to do what he could to help her close the case on her assault. Then maybe she could finally begin to really trust again. He felt she was holding off a piece of herself from him, some small portion that told him she didn't completely believe he would never hurt her. Of course, it didn't help that he had a child to suddenly appear out of nowhere.

"So, tell me about why you're here," Kathie said.

He swallowed the last bite of his cookie and took a drink of the coffee. It was nearly as good as the cookie and he wondered how a pot of black coffee could taste different, depending on who made it.

"I'm here because my fiancée needs to find someone," he said.

"Distant relative? Parent?"

"No, not exactly. They aren't related by blood."

Kathie looked perplexed. "Then how do you think I can help?"

"We have the DNA, and, *so* far, we've been able to find a fourth cousin of the man she's looking for. We met the cousin, but they don't want to help us go any further."

"Hmm. That makes it more complicated. Using genetic genealogy to identify someone can be sensitive work, but using the name of the cousin I can try to build a family tree. Have you already tried that?"

"No, that's why I'm here. I can help and I'm a fast learner, but I don't know where to go from here," Sam said.

Kathie leaned back in her chair, crossing her arms over her lap.

"There's some easy first steps we can take. Easy, but time-consuming. Things like searching online for obituaries on which the cousin is listed, then taking the other names of family members and run them, try to start building it by generations, and see how they connect with each other. Do you know where the fourth cousin lives, or are we looking worldwide?"

"A few relatives of the fourth cousin live in Mercer County, West Virginia," he said, opening his binder and shuffling through a few papers until he found the one with the names listed.

"That's a start. How did you find that?" she asked.

"Facebook." Sam felt silly talking about a social media platform as though it played an important part in anything. In this, it was a necessary evil but, in general, he wasn't a fan of how people were able to get into one another's business so easily through all the new technology. It was a good thing he kept his head under the hood of a car most of the time and didn't have time for getting into that kind of mess.

"Facebook can be a great tool," Kathie said. "I tell you what, why don't you leave the data with me and let me see what I can dig up."

"I'd appreciate that, but first we should probably talk about your fee."

"I don't know if I'm going to take the case yet. I'd like to spend some time looking at it, then I'll let you know. I won't charge you anything for the preliminary analysis and I'll let you know before I go too far."

Sam passed the papers over to her side of the table. "I appreciate any help you can give us, Mrs. Huff."

She laughed and waved her hand in the air. "Please—don't call me Mrs. Huff. It makes me feel ancient. Kathie is fine. Before you go, would you like some of my jarred treats? I've got jelly and Pico de Gallo. Jalapenos too if you're a spicy kind of man."

He grinned at her. "I guess we need to ask my fiancée that question."

"I can see you really care about her," Kathie said when she finished chuckling. "Or you wouldn't be here today."

"Yeah, I do." He looked down at his feet and got quiet. "I just hope she knows how much. We've had a bit of a rough spot because of something in my past suddenly popping up. I just want to be able to do this one thing for her."

Kathie reached over and put her hand on his. "Sometimes it can be hard to figure things out when it comes to relationships, but you are showing her you are willing to do the hard stuff. You know it's love when the happiness of another person is essential to your own."

"That sounds about right. If only I could make her see how much I care."

"She probably does, even if she doesn't say it. Some people tend to only accept the love they think they deserve, based on what life experiences they've had. But commitment and time goes a long way to breaking through walls they put up."

She was wise, he'd give her that. Her words almost made tears come up.

He stood, smiling at her.

Kaiser growled at him. It was a funny little growl, but Sam wouldn't press his luck. He took a step back. "Thank you so much for seeing me today, Kathie. And I'll take that offer of the Pico De Gallo and a jar of jelly, if you have enough to spare."

"Oh, do I have enough! I could probably hand it out to the whole town if I wanted. I'll send you home with my famous Strawberry Champagne jelly as well as the Bubbly Berry. Get that girl of yours to make you some homemade biscuits to slather it on in the morning. But stop and get you some tortillas and that Pico will be a good treat for sitting in front of a nice movie tonight with your sweetheart."

She went to the shelf and pulled several jars from it, then brought them to Sam.

"Wow. Thanks for all this. And for your help with the research, Kathie. I hope we can find our man."

Kathie smiled at him confidently. "If he's out there, I'll find him."

CHAPTER 7

*T*aylor knocked twice, then opened the door to Faire Tinsley's house and walked in. The grand staircase, always an imposing focal point, had the wall leading upstairs transformed into a stunning display of paintings. Her eyes scanned the room, taking in the vibrant colors and intricate details of the artwork that adorned every wall, all of it different than the traditional pieces that used to be there. She was glad to see that the historic charm of the house still lingered, preserved in its architecture, but now intertwined with the creativity of Faire's work.

As Taylor marveled at the transformation, Lucy came flying around the corner. Her ponytailed hair disheveled and sweat glistening on her brow, a hammer in her hand. She looked like an adorable pixie fairy with her overalls and tank top, her feet stuck into simple, white canvas shoes. It was clear that she had been working hard to make Faire's upcoming debut as an artist a success, and Taylor couldn't help but be impressed, especially considering—that she knew of—Lucy had never worked in the creative arts field. She looked so confident in what she was doing. So happy.

It was a new look for her, and Taylor approved.

"Taylor, you made it!" Lucy greeted her with a tired but genuine smile. Her dog, Ginger, was right behind her, tail wagging up a storm.

"Yeah, I couldn't miss this preview," Taylor replied, wrapping her sister in a warm hug. "Where's Faire?

"She had to take her crazy bird to get his beak trimmed. She'll be back later, and hopefully the snip will make him stop talking so much."

Taylor laughed. "When is the big reveal?"

Johnny came around the corner and hollered in glee to see her. Taylor picked him up and twirled him around the big hall, making him throw his head back and laugh. He had a way of making her forget about everything bad in the world with just one giggle.

"He just ate half a bag of jellybeans so don't make him throw up. The showing is next month. Don't worry. I'll remind you," Lucy said. "Come on. I'll show you around."

Taylor put Johnny down and let Lucy guide her through the rooms, stopping and explaining some of the best pieces. Faire communicated with the deceased and turns out she has a unique talent for capturing the connections between those who have passed on and their loved ones still on Earth.

One particular piece caught Taylor's eye immediately.

It depicted the faces of a father and adult son looking down from the corner of the canvas, both of whom had tragically died together, reaching out toward a woman sitting in a rocking chair in a tiny garden. There was snow on the ground and frosting the tops and tips of the various plants. The emotions conveyed in the painting were palpable—the longing, the love, and the desire to bridge the gap between life and death. A row of fir trees was lined up in the background in neat rows, but next to the woman was one very small birch tree decorated with tiny, red sparrow ornaments. She gazed at it with a look of melancholy.

Taylor recognized the family portrayed in the painting all too well; she had worked their case as a detective and knew them intimately.

"That's incredible," Taylor whispered, her voice catching. Faire had captured the kindness and wisdom in Amos' eyes perfectly. And his son, David, looked like he could jump out of the screen. "You know I worked that case, right? Those are the Higgins from out at the Christmas tree farm. Beverly is going to buy that piece."

"Unless Danny beats her to it." Lucy nodded, her eyes misting up. "See what I was telling you? Faire has a real gift, and her art truly is going to bring comfort to those who've lost someone dear."

"I agree. I'm so glad this was all discovered while she's still alive to enjoy the fanfare." She looked at a few more framed pieces before turning back to Lucy. "By the way, Shane mentioned you two went on a date," she said, raising an eyebrow.

Lucy's cheeks turned slightly pink as she fidgeted with a nearby collage. "Oh, yeah. I meant to tell you about that."

Taylor couldn't hide her annoyance. "Why didn't you? Don't you think it's weird that Shane used to have a thing for me, and now he's suddenly focused on you?"

Lucy sighed, her gaze shifting to the floor. "I know it's strange, but it just happened. And besides, I flirted with him first. He's not to blame in this."

Taylor couldn't argue with that, but she couldn't help but bring up another point. "You know Corbin's interested in you too, right? I think you should consider him. He's a genuinely nice guy."

"And so is Shane." Lucy narrowed her eyes at Taylor. "What is the big deal? Maybe you really do want Shane for yourself?"

Taylor felt her cheeks get warm.

"Don't be ridiculous. There was never anything between me and Shane and there never will be." She turned away.

Lucy gave her a knowing wink. "Oh, really? Come on, big sister. Not even in high school? I seem to remember you being kind of possessive about him around me and the girls."

"It was one kiss, Lucy. Nothing more. We were friends, and, I can tell you right now, he's not your type. Too serious and by the book. Corbin is more your style. Not Shane."

Lucy looked conflicted, her thoughts seemingly torn between Shane and Corbin. Before she could respond, Johnny pulled at her legs.

"Shane, Shane, Shane," he repeated, like a parrot.

Lucy watched Johnny for a moment, a smile tugging at her lips. "Well, looks like Johnny's casting his vote for who should date whom," she quipped, trying to lighten the mood.

Taylor chuckled, her shoulders relaxing. "Yeah, sounds about right. You taking advice from a toddler. But, hey, I need to run. Speaking of the devil, I have to meet him in half an hour. I'll tell him you send your love."

She was teasing—and Lucy laughed—but Taylor only pretended to smile.

Something about thinking of Shane with her little sister didn't sit well with her.

⁂

TAYLOR HATED this part of her job more than anything. When she had to look family survivors of a tragedy straight in the eye, and ask them painful questions, it was gut-wrenching. But it was also a necessary evil.

Shane clicked record on his small micro recorder and set it on the coffee table. He had been a few minutes late due to interviewing a few of Bishop's golf partners—who all claimed that Bishop would never cheat on his wife—and he wanted to get started quickly.

Abby sat as close to her brother, Larson, as she could get on the couch.

Their Aunt Edith supervised from the other end.

"Tell us one more time, Abby. What happened that night before you went up to your brother's room?" Shane asked.

He'd sensed her discomfort and had picked up the ball when it came to questions directed at Abby. Taylor just couldn't do it. She was so young and sad.

Abby took her fingers from her mouth. Her aunt had told them she'd regressed into several behaviors she'd left behind as a toddler. That was to be expected.

"I heard a scream from outside my window and it woke me up," she said.

"Did the scream sound like it was from anyone you know?" Shane asked.

She nodded solemnly and her fingers made their way back to her mouth. "Mama."

Larson winced beside her, but he pushed her hand down so she could talk clearly.

"Then what happened?" Shane asked.

"I was scared but I got up and went to the window."

"What did you see?"

Her lip quivered before she answered, then she looked up and straight at Shane. "I saw a man walking away. I think he had an axe over his shoulder."

"Abby, can you tell us what he looked like?" Shane asked softly.

She shook her head, her eyes big and round. "No. But he was tall."

"How tall?" Shane asked, standing up. "As tall as me?"

"Yes," she said, nodding again.

"Hmm. That's really tall," Shane said. "Larson, please stand up next to me."

Larson looked uncomfortable but he stood and positioned himself beside Shane. He was tall, but not as tall.

"Now, Abby. Think about it. Was the man as tall as me, or like your brother?"

Abby looked from Shane to Larson, then back.

Larson crossed his arms over his chest. "Was he tall like me or tall like Marc, Abby? The detective is about Marc's height."

Abby pointed at Shane.

"It was dark," the aunt said. "I'm not sure she's a very reliable witness."

"That's fine," Taylor said. "We just want to get her thinking and maybe something will come back."

Edith shook her head angrily. "She doesn't need to be thinking of this. She needs to move on and forget it."

"Once we wrap up the case, there won't be any more questions from us," Taylor said. "And I'm sure that you are getting them some counseling lined up, yeah?"

The aunt looked perturbed that Taylor had circled it back to her.

"What did you do next, Abby?" Shane asked, moving the interview along.

"I took my blanket and went upstairs to wake up Larson." She sat back against the couch and put her fingers back in her mouth, a sign she was done talking.

"Okay, Larson. You take it from here. Tell us every little detail you can think of," Taylor said.

He sighed, then began. "I don't know what time it was. Somewhere between midnight and two o'clock, I guess. I woke up to her standing beside my bed. I sat up and asked her what was wrong. She said she saw a man outside. I told her she was having a nightmare and to get in bed with me. She did."

"Does she have a history of nightmares?" Taylor asked.

"Yes. We all do. Ever been in foster care?" Larson said pointedly, his expression sarcastic.

"Then what happened?" Shane asked.

"We went to sleep. The next morning about seven, I went downstairs and didn't see my folks, so I looked out the kitchen window to see if they were outside. I saw my mom lying there. I called 911. That's it."

"Would they normally be outside at that time of day?" Taylor asked.

He shrugged. "Sometimes. My mom waters her flowers and stuff."

"Why didn't you search the rest of the house first?" Shane asked.

"Because I expected Mom to be in the kitchen making breakfast. When she wasn't, I looked out the window. That's it."

"You didn't wonder where your dad was when you saw your mom lying there?" Shane asked. "Maybe think to call out for him?"

Larson looked confused. "I don't know. After I saw my mom lying there naked, all I could think of was to get her help. 911 seemed like the right thing to do."

"They've been taught to call emergency services since they were little. That's exactly what we would expect them to do," Edith said. "Kim needed help. Larson tried to get it there. What is so hard to figure out in that formula? I think we're done here."

"We appreciate you letting us talk to them," Taylor said, coming to a stand.

"One last thing," Shane said. "We need you to bring Larson down to the department for a DNA swab and handprints."

Edith turned red in the face. "Goodness Almighty. Why would you need that?"

"It's just protocol," Shane said, his tone friendly and cool. "Then he can be eliminated from any suspect lists."

"Fine. But it won't be today. I have too many things already on my calendar. I'll get him there next week," Edith said. "Their mental health is my priority right now, not helping you solve your case."

Taylor thought that was a strange statement, considering Kimberly was her sister. She followed Shane outside and to his car.

Next stop, the behavioral health center.

She and Shane were going to get admitted, locked up, then try to break out.

CHAPTER 8

*S*am rubbed the knot on his head and cursed the tiny Mini Cooper he was working on. It felt like playing with a Tonka toy, and he needed to twist his body in all sorts of ways to get in and under all the places he needed to be to take out the cracked radiator and install a new one. He'd busted his head at least twice on the hood just trying to look a few inches further.

Why anyone would want to drive one of these things was beyond him. One accident and it would fold up like an accordion. A casket with a motor. He'd said as much to the owner and been immediately told how wrong he was, that the Mini Cooper had received good ratings as one of the safest small cars on the road.

Depended on who was doing the rating, he supposed. Normally he wouldn't have accepted the job on such a frustratingly small car, seeing how he was a big guy who didn't like tight spaces. However, the owner was paying him well to do it, and what he made on the Mini Cooper would be going toward paying Kathie Huff for whatever fee she decided on. He wanted to cover all of it himself. It was his idea to bring on a professional genealogist, and he'd pay for every penny.

"Come on, boy," he waved at Diesel, who had sat there all morning grinning at him every time he cussed out loud.

They went inside and he grabbed a biscuit from the pan still sitting on the stove. They were canned, but, with Kathie's strawberry champagne jelly slathered inside, they tasted gourmet. He was on his fifth of the morning and would have to do some extra pushups to make up for it.

His phone rang and he pulled it from his pocket and looked.

Unknown number.

"Hello?"

"Sam," a woman's voice said.

He felt a jolt of anxiety because he recognized her voice immediately. It was still low and husky. Sounded like she'd never given up her smoking habit.

"Brooke. Thanks for calling." He immediately started pacing the kitchen.

"Yeah ... Alice is in a lot of trouble. I'm so sorry she contacted you. I've straightened her out and you shouldn't hear from her again."

He stopped and leaned against the sink. "Wait? No—I didn't want her to be in trouble. It's fine. I just—"

"—Sam. Stop talking. She's not your kid. I don't know why she got that crazy idea into her head. You remember Derek? Well, she belongs to him. They don't get along. Never have, but that's his fault. He didn't want kids then and he don't want them now. Which is unfortunate because we have two more under five years old. But that's a family problem and has nothing to do with you. Good thing I make my own money. Can't depend on his sorry ass."

He ran his hands through his hair. He didn't know if he felt relieved or disappointed. Maybe both. He felt a little sorry for Brooke. She sounded defeated.

"Oh. Okay," he said. "I think she found my letter and

compared the dates or something like that. Please don't be mad at her. She sounds like a great kid."

He could hear Brooke sigh on the other end.

"Sometimes. When she's not overthinking everything. I took her phone and she's grounded now. She can't be reaching out to strangers on the internet. This could've ended badly if you weren't such a nice guy."

"Oh, wow. You're right. I didn't think about that. Jeez. I hope she's learned her lesson. There's a lot of weirdos out there."

"Oh, she's learning her lesson. You can bet on that," Brooke said. "She's getting a little too big for her britches and I took her down a notch or two."

Sam felt worried again for Alice but what could he say?

Diesel was staring up at him and whined, sensing Sam's uncomfortable vibes.

"How's Josh doing?" He asked instead. "Haven't talked to him in ages."

"Neither have I. I don't stay in contact with my family anymore. Too toxic. They never wanted to help me when I was in dire straits, and I won't forget it. What about you? Your family okay?"

"Yeah, just my Dad and I now. Mom's been gone a while. I got engaged, too," he said. He wasn't sure why he added that in, but it slipped out.

There was a long pause.

"Congrats, I guess," Brooke said, though her tone was anything but congratulatory. "I'll never get married. Don't need a ring on my finger to make things official. Derek ain't the marrying type anyway. Makes it easier for him to up and leave when he gets a wild hair."

"I—yeah," he didn't know what the proper response was to a statement like that. "Well, thank you again for calling. Sorry for the trouble."

"It's fine. Not your fault. Alice needs to keep her nose in her own business and stay out of mine. I'm taking care of it. You have a nice life, Sam."

"Uh, yeah, you,—"

She didn't wait for his response before hanging up, and Sam stood there staring at the phone in his hand. Something just didn't sit right about that conversation.

He thought of Taylor and how relieved she was going to be that he wasn't already a father. But then he thought of Alice and imagined how disappointed she was that the man she didn't want to be her father actually is, and the one she wanted isn't.

Brooke was always a ball buster, and she was probably just as tough as a mother. He hoped that she wasn't too hard on Alice. Funny, but, when he pictured her, it was never as a mom to three kids. From what he remembered, she was a hard-shell type of girl, kind of selfish, too. Not one you'd think would have a maternal bone in her body. But what did he know? Lots of tough girls grew up to be great mothers.

He looked down at Diesel.

"Ready to get back to work, buddy?"

Diesel's tail thumped the floor rapidly.

"Git up, lazy. We've got to finish getting the Magoo car on the road so I can do some internet sleuthing tonight, or your mom might be busting my balls, too."

※

TAYLOR WITHDREW HER GUN, unloaded it, and took it to the safe that Sam had installed when she'd started spending more nights there. Now that Lucy and Johnny were staying with her in the cabin, she tried to stay out of their hair as much as possible. The few weeks that she wasn't talking to Sam because of the Alice revelation had been difficult. With only seven hundred square feet in her little home at the farm, it was easy to get on each other's nerves.

She was going to have to decide what to do soon about the living arrangements.

Carefully she released her belt and laid it on the side table. She was exhausted. Even though she was investigating the Swanson case with Shane, she'd still had to do her turn at school traffic. Some lughead had decided to blaze through the school crossing doing fifty miles an hour just as the kids were coming out. She'd chased him all the way to county line before he'd finally pulled over. Turned out to be a senior citizen who reeked of Jack Daniels. By the time she'd finished processing him, she'd put fourteen hours on the clock for the day.

Two of those were spent in a locked-down room at the behavioral health center after they'd left Edith's house. She and Shane had tried to jimmy the door, pry the window, and do everything short of kicking their way out of the room. Shane was pissed when he'd finally had to call the girl at the desk to tell her they were ready for her to open the door. His macho ego was bruised, evidently.

Their conclusion was that if Marc had left his room that night, it would've only been because someone let him out. And—so far—everyone claimed to have been on top of all their charges with no off head counts.

That means Marc would've had to leave undetected, but the staff said it was impossible. After their experiment, Taylor would have to agree.

She removed her shoes and put her foot over her knee, rubbing it through the aching sole to reenergize it. She was beat. One silver lining was that, because of the seriousness of the case, she'd been let off the farm duties for now. Cate, Jo, Anna, and Lucy were covering her chores. For how much longer Taylor wasn't sure, and she felt bad about not doing her share. It helped that Eldon was spending more time at the farm with Jo and Levi and was learning the ropes, too.

But thank God she had the best fiancé in the county.

As soon as she had a quick shower, she was meeting him in the kitchen to eat homemade pizza. He'd decided that he was going to learn to cook because—and these were his words—*it wasn't fair for all of it to fall on her when they got married.*

She hoped he was adding a fresh salad, but, if not, she wasn't complaining.

"He's a good daddy, isn't he?" she crooned to Diesel as she went to the bathroom, got undressed, then stepped under the scalding water.

She tried to clear her mind, but little Abby's sad face kept monopolizing her thoughts. She wondered what would happen to her and Larson. Aunt Edith was nice to take them in, but she was a bit strange, and Taylor had a gut feeling it wasn't going to work out for long term.

She poured shampoo into her hand and then began working it in while she thought over the case details they knew so far. But she was so tired her mind couldn't put them in the neat order she usually catalogued things.

Maul. Found in the woods and is definitely the murder weapon but was wiped clean.

Stabbing weapon not found.

Bloody palm print. Partial. Doesn't belong to either victim.

No indication of extramarital affairs.

Nothing in the house was taken.

With the shampoo rinsed, she started the conditioning. Tonight, her hair would smell like tangerines. Sam loved her shampoo, and she loved the way he put his nose all through her hair and around her neck when her hair was freshly washed.

Shane said the handprint had been sent to the FBI lab in Washington, D.C. Being only a partial, it was too complicated for just any lab to process. They still needed to get prints from both Marc and Larson, to eliminate them.

The door opened and Sam peeked behind the shower curtain.

"You coming? I thought you passed out in here."

"Sorry. I'm rinsing now. Give me ten."

He ogled her until she pulled the curtain closed again and told him to get lost.

She stopped obsessing about the case and quickly shaved her legs, washed in all the right places, then turned off the water and wrapped herself in a towel. After slathering on some moisturizer and combing through her wildly wet hair, she threw on some joggers and one of Sam's soft T-shirts and followed the scent of pizza to the kitchen.

Sam didn't have a dining room. Well, he had one, but he used it for his office now and she sat at the kitchen table where he'd lit two candlesticks.

He plated the pizza and salad, then brought them to the table along with a bottle of dressing. He already had two tall glasses of ice water waiting.

"It smells delicious," Taylor said.

"*You* smell delicious."

"Thanks. But back to the pizza. I can only have one piece. All this cooking you're doing is going to make it impossible to find a decent wedding dress."

"Aww—it makes me happy when you talk like that." Sam grinned and sat down.

"About gaining weight?"

He looked stricken. "No. About *wedding* plans."

She laughed.

He lifted his glass. "A toast before we start."

"Okay, what're we toasting?" she held hers up.

"Two things."

"Okay ..." she said, holding her glass in mid-air.

"I bought a gun and have already gone through two safety classes."

She barely moved. "Why all of a sudden? And why not ask me to help?"

"Because I wanted to surprise you. You kept telling me I

needed to do it, and I kept putting it off. Now you don't have to be the only one to carry."

She couldn't say much to that. She had encouraged him to take a gun class and get comfortable with weapons, then to buy one. She would've liked to have been there to help him pick out his first gun, but that wasn't a hill she was ready to die on. She'd ask him more about it when she had more energy—including what gun he bought.

"Okay. Congrats. But I'm not the only one in my family who carries a gun. My dad carries one and just about everyone has one in their home for emergencies. Georgia is in the top ten of the most gun-friendly states. What's the second thing?"

"The fact that I'm not a father." He wiggled his eyebrows at her. "Yet."

Taylor set her glass down with a loud thump.

"What? What do you mean?"

He put his glass down, too. "I talked to Alice's mom today. She said I'm not the dad and she doesn't know why or how Alice got that in her head. She apologized and that's that."

"Well, that was an abrupt end to your fatherhood. How do you feel about it?"

Sam shrugged. "I'm glad I'm not a dad yet, but I feel sorry for Alice. Her mom said she was being punished. I hope she's not too hard on her."

Taylor took a long drink of water, then sat back in her chair. "I remember when Lucy was twelve. She wouldn't listen to me! I thought I'd lose my mind, and to help me figure it all out I did a report in my Biology class on what happens to a twelve-year-old's body psychologically and physically to make them so hard to deal with. Turns out that—at age twelve—parts of our brains are still developing. There's something called the prefrontal cortex that controls things like problem solving and impulse control. It's not developed yet at twelve. It also accounts for the area that helps with decision-making and thinking about consequences. I'm sure Alice wasn't really thinking about the *what if you weren't really her dad* scenario."

"Well, that helps make sense a little," he said, but he still looked sad. "She was so excited that she'd found me. I wonder how she took the news."

Taylor wondered if maybe a small part of him wasn't so happy that Alice wasn't his.

"Probably not well. Her body is producing an overload of hormones that play havoc with emotions, giving preteens more mood swings and making them unpredictable. I know that Lucy had me pulling my hair out. I started sleeping in the living room just to make sure she didn't sneak out the front door but, half the time, I wanted to throw her out it."

"I think that was just Lucy, and nothing about being twelve," Sam said, laughing. "She's still that way, isn't she? She doesn't like being told what to do, she has no impulse control, and she has mood swings. Boom."

"Good point," Taylor said, thinking again about Lucy and Shane. She just couldn't imagine them on a date. She planned to tell Sam about that, too, but not tonight. It felt like he needed to talk about Alice.

"Alice didn't talk like a bratty pre-teen. She wasn't sarcastic. Had some great manners, too. I know I haven't met her in person, but she seemed like a nice kid."

Taylor reached out and covered Sam's hand with hers. She could see that he was upset.

"You will be a wonderful dad one day, Sam. Just the way you've handled this thing proves that to me. You could've freaked out, hung up on Alice and never spoke to her again, but you didn't. You were going to do the right thing."

He sighed. "Yeah. I was. But that's done. How was your day?"

"Not great. I really don't want to rehash it right now. Let's eat and, if you have any news from Kathie, I'd love to hear it."

"Okay, but let's toast for real this time. To us. For whatever it is for now, and what it will be in the future."

They clinked glasses and Taylor picked up her pizza and took a big bite. Her eyes nearly rolled back in her head from the fast signals of delicious flavors that hit her tongue. She chewed quickly.

"You rocked this pizza, Sam. I don't even know how to make pizza from scratch."

He beamed around his own slice, the smile reaching to his eyes.

When he put it down, he wiped his mouth. "Oh. Kathie called me this afternoon. She's still working on building the family tree based on the fourth cousin we found. Once the leaves start compiling on the branches, she'll be able to identify common ancestors between the cousin and the unknown male."

"Like brothers and uncles?" Taylor poked at her salad. In theory, sticking mostly to salad sounded like the best decision, but she wanted more pizza.

"She said most likely she'll find great-great-great grandparents or further back first. Then she'll start tracing those to present day descendants."

"That's when we'll start really getting somewhere," she said.

"Yep. I'll be able to help her more, too. Kathie said we'll be poring over historical records like census data, birth certificates, marriage certificates, and all that. She's going to give us a huge discount because I'm going to assist."

"How did I get so lucky to find you?" Taylor said. "I sure don't deserve you."

He winked. "Oh, yes, you do. And I'm not that wonderful. You're going to research obituaries. Too depressing for me."

Taylor laughed. She had more experience with death than he did. Sam didn't even like to watch scary movies. His weekend picks were Disney stuff half the time.

"I can do that." She'd find the time somewhere.

Sam was suddenly serious. "We're going to find him, Taylor. I won't give up until we do. Then, when this is done, you're going to stand up there and marry me. Right?"

"Of course. But you finding him doesn't have anything to do with me marrying you."

"I know that, but I've decided that, until you are free of this mystery, and free of him, I won't have all of you. We're going to do this together, then start our new life together by putting it in the past."

Taylor wished she hadn't just taken another bite of pizza. The sudden tears in her throat almost caused her to choke.

Sam was wrong.

She really didn't deserve someone as wonderful as him.

He saw her struggling and smiled. "Hey, don't forget about dessert."

"Don't you hear a thing I say? Dress? Remember?" she joked. "I'm already cheating with pizza. I won't be having dessert. But, just for fun, what are *you* having?"

"You. Good thing you didn't want none."

CHAPTER 9

A week into the investigation, the Catholic church stood still as the hushed murmurs of the gathered mourners filled the air. The somber atmosphere was only broken by the soft, rhythmic repetition of the Rosary, prayed by those seeking intercession from Mary for the souls of Kimberly and Bishop Swanson.

In the front pew of the church, the three surviving children sat together, a picture of sorrow and loss. Marc sat on one end, his gaze focused on the floor in front of him. Judith Maloney, the advocate they'd met at the facility sat next to him, most likely his official escort. Larson was on the other side, offering a quiet yet reassuring presence. Next, Abby, the youngest of the siblings, found solace under the protective arm of her Aunt Edith. A couple others were next to Edith, but Taylor didn't know who they were.

She stood inconspicuously in the back of the church, Shane beside her. They had spent the earliest part of the day doing Zoom interviews with the two women who had filed police reports on Bishop Swanson when he'd harassed them in the parking lot of the abortion clinic they'd visited. Both were shocked at the news of his death, and both had solid alibis. Neither Taylor nor Shane thought they had any part in the crime.

The eyes of the townspeople—or at least those that she could see from her position—darted toward the front pew where the Swanson boys sat. Unspoken suspicion lingered in the air, as many obviously feared and believed that the killer was among them.

Taylor leaned toward Shane and whispered softly, "Look at the people here, Shane. They can't stop looking at the boys."

Shane nodded in agreement.

The people could be right, that Marc was guilty, but she had every intention of giving the case a fair and impartial investigation.

Her gaze scanned the congregation. Among the mourners, a few individuals drew her attention for various reasons. There was Donald Logano and his wife, the Swanson's neighbors that she and Shane had met. His wife kept stealing furtive glances at Marc while clutching a rosary tightly, her face etched with an unreadable expression.

Then there was Tina, Kimberly's teacher bestie. She seemed overly interested in the Swanson boys, her curiosity bordering on intrusive and rude.

And finally, Clayton Davis, Kimberly's principal at the high school, who appeared oddly detached from the proceedings. His gaze frequently shifted toward the caskets, betraying an unsettling fascination.

As the Mass commenced, the congregation solemnly followed the rituals and prayers. The offering of Christ's Body and Blood, a memorial of His death, served as a poignant reminder that, even in death, Kimberly and Bishop Swanson were still a part of the Body of Christ.

Communion followed, with Marc, Abby, and Larson taking part, along with most of the attendees. Taylor and Shane noticed a few individuals who abstained, realizing that they might not be Catholic.

The priest, standing resolute at the ornate altar, commanded the attention of the hushed congregation. He was a tall man, his lean figure draped in his flowing robes. The pallor of his complexion suggested years spent worshiping inside the church.

His salt-and-pepper hair, neatly combed and meticulously styled, framed a face that radiated a stern demeanor. His eyes, a piercing shade of steel gray, held the weight of the world and seemed to penetrate the souls of those who met his gaze.

As he delivered his homily and eulogy, his deep voice filled the vast space of the church. His admonishments against materialism were stern, his words directed primarily toward the youth of the congregation. He spoke with an unwavering belief in the importance of serving God, his message resounding with the promise of heavenly rewards. In heaven, he proclaimed, the roads were paved in gold, and everyone lived in mansions.

At that, Taylor caught Shane grimacing and rolling his eyes toward the ceiling.

She observed the next rituals, with her thoughts a whirlwind. The symbols, chants, and ceremonies seemed foreign to her, and she couldn't help but find the proceedings a mix of solemn and bizarre. She'd been to church plenty when she was a kid, always with her sisters, following Della Ray like a line of baby chicks. Any foster child under Della Ray's roof was required to accompany her to Sunday morning and Wednesday night services, but always in a Baptist church, which was vastly different than what she was witnessing here.

"It's all so strange," she murmured to Shane. "The candles, the smoke, the repeated kneeling. It feels like an elaborate theater production."

Shane nodded in agreement. "And the focus on suffering and repentance, rather than celebrating or remembering the Swansons."

She knew that beneath the layers of tradition and ritual were stories and secrets, some that might even lead them to the truth behind the brutal murders that had shaken their town. The power of a secret, as she well knew, could be the igniter of evil that could permeate through a group of people, even if only starting with one. Secrets were a malicious tool of power to those who kept them and those who held the power to expose them.

As the service continued, Taylor continued to observe the curious rituals and practices. Some of the hymns were comforting, and her outside perspective relaxed and allowed her to see the ceremony in a different light. She found herself feeling comfort as she watched the solemn communion, the chanting, and the repeated crossing of oneself before approaching the altar.

The psalm scripture reading and the eulogy followed, the priest's words fading into the background as Taylor's mind wandered, her thoughts filled with the grisly crime scene. Bishop's seventeen stab wounds, and Kimberly's seven, plus her split skull.

She hoped that whatever or wherever it was that Catholics went to next, it was more than enough to make up for Bishop and Kim's tragic last moments on earth.

CHAPTER 10

*S*am's nerves were up again as he parked his car on the cobblestone street in historic downtown. Common Grounds coffee shop was nestled between the towering facades of older buildings, a quaint little place that seemed to defy the march of time. Its weathered brick exterior, adorned with ivy climbing up the walls, gave it an almost fairytale quality. Tucked away in this picturesque setting, it was a haven for the people of Hart's Ridge to get away and take a breath—and a sip.

Next door and attached was a tiny place called The Farmer's Daughter, its cozy interior spilling over with home cooked meals, baked goods, and various gift items. The tantalizing aroma of casseroles and other oven-ready delights wafted out of the open door, instantly reminding Sam of his grandmother's kitchen from his childhood. He'd been in there before to grab a meal to take home, and he'd probably do it again.

As he pushed through the heavy wooden door of the coffee shop, a brass bell tinkled overhead, signaling his arrival. The interior was dimly lit with warm, soft lighting, casting a soft, amber glow over the worn, hardwood floors. The walls were adorned with local artwork, each piece a bright and interesting addition to the room. To the side of the high tables with stools, a set of weathered, overstuffed, leather reading chairs gave the space a cozy and eclectic vibe.

The air was filled with the comforting scent of freshly brewed coffee, an intoxicating aroma to greet visitors.

Sam scanned the room, spotting Kathie at a corner table near the large window. She was sipping a cup of black coffee, steam rising from the porcelain mug. A small stack of papers sat beside her.

He approached, offering a warm smile as he pulled out a chair. "Hey, Kathie."

She looked up from her coffee, her face breaking into a grin. "Sam, good to see you again. Have a seat."

He settled into the chair and looked up at the menu on the wall. "You too. I appreciate you meeting me."

"Of course," she said. "Before we start, do you want to grab you a coffee?"

"I already had my coffee today, so I think I'll try one of their green citrus smoothies," he said. "Trying to get my superfoods in for the day."

Kathie chuckled. "You a health-conscious kind of guy?"

He shrugged. "Sometimes. It can't hurt."

"You have to go up and order," she said.

Sam went to the counter, where an antique cash register sat atop a worn, wooden counter. He gave his order to the barista, who skillfully prepared his green citrus smoothie. While he waited, he couldn't resist the temptation to explore the adjoining shop, The Farmer's Daughter.

Stepping through the arched doorway, he found himself surrounded by the nostalgic ambiance of a bygone era. The chalkboard menu displayed an array of mouthwatering options for the week, including creamy shrimp casserole, decadent steak with chimichurri sauce, and rosemary chicken with grapes and garlic sauce. The thought of a home cooked meal from this place brought back cherished memories of his grandmother's comforting dishes.

He gazed through the glass door of the freezer, where neatly labeled dinners promised convenience. All it would take was twenty minutes in the oven, and he could have a delicious meal ready for Taylor when she got home from work. Perhaps a small way to make her day a little brighter.

They called his name from the counter, and he strolled back through, making note to grab a meal on the way out. If Taylor worked late, he could have it warming in the oven for when she got home.

He returned to the table with Kathie, setting his green citrus smoothie down in front of him. As he sipped the cool blend of banana, orange, and spinach, sending a refreshing wave through him, Kathie got straight to the point. "I've made some progress on the case."

Sam leaned forward, eager for any news. "That's great to hear. What have you found?"

She took a sip of her coffee, then began to explain. "First, I've been working on eliminating unlikely matches. This helps us narrow down our focus. I've also been utilizing public genealogy databases, like GEDmatch and FamilySearch, to find additional matches and expand the family tree."

He nodded, feeling overwhelmed at everything she was saying. It sounded complicated.

"Furthermore," she continued, "I've been building a profile of potential suspects based on age, location, and other pertinent details."

Sam's excitement started to bubble within him. The idea that they might finally be getting closer to finding the person responsible for Taylor's assault was almost too good to be true.

Kathie's tone turned more serious as she went on. "Now, here's where it gets interesting. I've identified four possible male leads. However, they're all siblings, and we'll need to narrow it down further. This might prove to be a bit challenging."

"Four leads," Sam repeated, his heart pounding in his chest. "That's incredible."

Kathie nodded. "But the next steps will require some careful investigation."

"Where do you think they are?

"We can't be sure yet, but, by researching home and land purchases, it seems that a few of them may be located in Mercer County, West Virginia."

Sam's excitement grew even more. He knew where Mercer County was. It was in the heart of Appalachia on the southern border of West Virginia.

They were getting closer, and he couldn't wait to dive into this new phase of the search.

Kathie took a sip of her coffee and leaned in. "We'll need to gather more information, maybe even visit Mercer County if necessary. This won't be easy, Sam, but the way that things are moving so far makes me feel in my gut that we might just find the guy."

He was just about to thank her again when his phone dinged, indicating a message.

> Sam, I'm so sorry to bug you, but I have a real emergency. Please come. -Alice

THE SHERIFF'S department bustled with activity and Taylor sat at her desk and read through her notes. They had to be missing something in the Swanson case. Shane had built a shared worksheet for the facts, dates, and logged evidence, and her fingers danced across the keyboard as she logged in to bring it up.

As she waited for the information to load, the pause finally gave her a moment to catch her breath.

She glanced at the clock on the wall. It was nearly the lunch hour, though she wouldn't have time for a break today. She'd brought a few granola bars, and they would have to do. Just as she was about to take a sip of her lukewarm coffee, Sam's familiar face appeared over the wall of her bullpen.

"Sam, what are you doing here?" she couldn't contain her surprise. Sam had never come to the department.

He cleared his throat, looking out of place against the backdrop of so many uniforms and cubicles.

Penner heard the interaction and turned around. "Hi, Sam. Good to see you, buddy."

"You too." He lowered his head to get closer to Taylor. "Dottie let me come back. Can you step outside? It's kind of important." He looked around, like he was afraid someone was listening.

Taylor frowned, momentarily puzzled. Setting her coffee aside, Taylor pushed her chair back and made her way out of the bullpen, heading for the nearest door to the parking lot.

"Sam, what's going on?" Taylor asked once they were outside.

Sam ran a hand through his hair, clearly agitated. "Alice called me. She's in trouble. I need to go to her."

Taylor's eyes widened with worry. "Trouble? What kind of trouble?"

"She didn't say, except to tell me no one is hurt. She sounded scared. She wants me to come to her house in North Carolina," Sam explained, his voice filled with urgency.

Taylor hesitated for a moment, considering the situation. "Sam, we should call the local emergency services in her area. They can handle this."

Sam shook his head, his determination unwavering. "I promised Alice that I would come personally. She trusts me, Taylor. I can't let her down."

"Where is her mother? You know she told you that Alice wouldn't contact you again."

"She's not there is all I know. I can't just not go. She sounded desperate."

Sighing, Taylor reluctantly agreed. "Alright, let me grab my things. We'll go together, but, if it's a dangerous situation, we call the authorities immediately. Deal?"

"Deal." She could see the relief settle over him immediately.

"Fine. Then we take the squad car. In case we need the lights."

They left the sheriff's department in a hurry, and, after Sam put the address in his phone, Taylor followed the directions, speeding down the country roads. The landscape transitioned from small towns to open fields and rolling hills, and the sun hung low in the sky, casting long shadows.

"Have you ever been to Murphy?" Taylor asked.

"No. I just know it's in North Carolina and they moved there a year ago." He squeezed his phone so hard that his knuckles were white. "Taylor, I know this is weird. She's not my kid and I've never even met her. But for some crazy reason, she trusts me."

"I know," Taylor said, her voice soft. "But I'm glad you picked me up. Anything could happen with you going there alone. She could say whatever she wanted, Sam, and you'd have no defense. Brooke could have you arrested. Have you thought of that?"

He didn't reply.

She continued. "When we get there, I'll assess the situation and make the call to the authorities. You have to let me do my job. Promise?"

"Only if it's something we can't handle, Taylor."

She nodded.

"I'm going to try to call her again," he said.

He dialed but the call went straight to voicemail, and she heard a muffled curse word escape his lips.

As they merged onto the interstate, the traffic became more

congested, and their journey slowed. Taylor's mind raced with worry for Alice, and she couldn't help but wonder what had prompted the young girl to reach out to Sam.

"Get off on this exit," Sam said.

Taylor saw a sign advertising private walking tours at a working cattle ranch, then a sign for Oconee white water rafting.

They were back in the country and, finally, after what felt like an eternity of driving, they arrived at their destination in a tiny neighborhood of no more than a dozen homes.

Alice's house itself looked like it could be nice but could use a coat of new paint and some yard work. The grass was high, and weeds framed the porch. A dozen or so small pairs of shoes lay in disarray on the steps next to pots with dead flowers.

Taylor parked the car, and they approached the front door.

Sam knocked and Taylor told him to step aside.

No one came.

This time Taylor knocked.

Loudly, while calling out. "Alice, are you in there?"

"Come in," they heard her call.

Taylor opened the door, her hand on her gun at her side, just in case.

The sight that greeted them was far from what Taylor had expected.

Alice stood in the living room, holding a toddler girl in her arms, while a diaper-clad toddler boy wailed at her feet. The place was in disarray, with toys scattered across the floor and an unmistakable feeling of chaos in the air.

Taylor smelled vomit and forced herself to breathe through her nose.

"I'm sorry," Alice said, breaking into tears. "They're sick. I don't have anything else to feed them and we are out of fever reducer, too."

"Where is your mother?" Sam asked.

There was no time for greetings or introductions, but Taylor noticed the way that Sam looked at Alice, a peculiar expression on his face that she couldn't read.

Alice shook her head. "I don't know. She's been gone for three days."

"And your dad?"

She shook her head again. "He's been gone longer. At least a week."

"Don't you have someone in your family you can call? A grandparent? Aunt or uncle?" Taylor asked.

"No." Alice said, looking embarrassed as she sniffled.

Social Services were going to have to be involved. Alice should be in school, and she wasn't old enough to have full supervision of toddlers, no matter how mature she was. Taylor felt rage brimming, thinking of Brooke and her partner, but she pushed it down. Now wasn't the time.

"We'll get things figured out," she said. "First things first."

"What do I do?" Sam said, looking helpless.

She immediately noticed that both children had flushed cheeks and sweaty foreheads. She approached them, her instincts kicking in.

Gently, she placed a hand on each child's forehead.

"They're feverish," she said. "We need to bring their temperatures down."

"I've tried," Alice said, looking worried. "I ran out of medicine yesterday."

Sam looked overwhelmed by the situation. "What can I do to help?"

"I'll handle them. You go to the nearest store," Taylor instructed, her mind racing as she assessed the situation. "We need fever reducer, Pedialyte, canned soup, and popsicles. And hurry," she urged, passing Sam the keys.

Without hesitation, Sam rushed out the door.

"Where do they take their baths?" Taylor asked, picking up the little boy.

"This way," Alice said, picking up the girl and heading down the hall to a small bathroom. It was decorated in a nature theme. Green rugs, froggy shower curtain, and lily pad paintings. One ceramic frog tissue holder on the back of the toilet. Three toothbrushes sat in the holder next to a soap dispenser, and an assortment of other toiletries were scattered about.

"I need to clean up in here before Mama comes home," Alice said.

"That's the least of our worries right now. Here, you sit right here and let me run your water," Taylor said, setting the boy on the toilet lid.

"I gave them baths yesterday but today they wouldn't let me," Alice said, sounding frantic. "I told them they'd feel better in the water."

"It's okay, Alice." Taylor bent down and turned on the water, adjusting it to lukewarm. "What's their names?"

"Hank and Honor," Alice said.

She sounded so tired and weak that Taylor put her hand on her forehead.

"You're burning up, too, Alice. As soon as you help me undress and get them in here, I want you to go to your mom's bathroom and run a bath, but don't use hot water. Keep it as lukewarm as you can stand. But not cold, either. Okay?"

Alice looked at her blankly. She looked exhausted. Her hair was greasy and straggly, and the tips of her ears were red.

"On second thought, I'll undress them." She took the little girl from her and pointed out the door. "You go ahead and take care of yourself."

"Okay," Alice said. "I just want to sleep a little bit first, though."

Taylor hated being the bad guy, but Alice was going to have to wait a bit before going to bed. "No, first a bath. Then you can help me get the kids dressed. When Sam gets here, I'll give you some medicine and then you can sleep."

"Was Sam mad that I called him?" Alice sat down on the floor in front of the vanity.

Her words cut Taylor to the quick. The girl was looking for acceptance. Sam was a stranger to her, but, in her mind, he was the father she wished she had.

"No, honey. He wasn't. But we can talk later, after everyone is cleaned up. You go ahead now, okay? We have a lot to do before everyone can settle in and get some rest."

Alice didn't argue anymore and, when she was gone, Taylor turned back to the two kids who looked up at her with wide eyes.

"Hi Honor. Hi Hank. I'm Taylor, and you know what? I have three little sisters! I used to give them baths all the time and I know how to make it fun. You ready?"

There was a bucket of toys next to the tub and Taylor plucked one out. It was a little red dinosaur.

The children looked up at her with wide eyes, their tiny voices filled with confusion. Taylor wished she'd have changed out of her uniform before coming.

"Where's Mama?" the little girl asked, her voice quivering.

Taylor's head was instantly filled with a picture of Abby, Honor's blue eyes replaced by Abby's dark ones. Abby would never see her mom again.

"What's his name?" Taylor asked, trying to divert their attention to the little toy. When they didn't answer, only staring at her, she made the creature dance along the rim of the bathtub. "If you don't want to tell me, I'll just call him Sir Farts A Lot."

They both laughed and then she knew she had them. It hadn't taken long. She hadn't lost her touch. She put more toys in the tub, using them to keep the kids entertained while she first washed their hair, then put the soap into their hands and told them to wash their bodies. She made a game out of rinsing them off, exclaiming over every bubble as she pretended to chase it off. She wanted to keep them in the water long enough to reset their body temperatures.

Soon they started looking sleepy.

She pulled the plug, letting the water go out, and then dried them as they stood there.

"Alice? Are you done?" she called out.

When Alice didn't reply, Taylor wrapped towels around both kids, then picked them up as bookends, her strong arms around them as she carried them down the hall.

"Let's go find your sister," she said. "She'll get your night-clothes for us."

She passed one room that obviously belonged to the two littles. The covers on the beds were tangled messes, but one was pink and the other blue. Toys littered the floor. She took them in and sat them down on a bed.

"Wait here for a minute. Let me check on Alice."

Quickly she went to the end of the hall, expecting to see another small bedroom but it was the primary room, and in the middle of the huge king-sized bed was Alice, fast asleep. She'd had a shower, and her hair was still wrapped in a towel, and she lay curled into a fetal position, the bathrobe barely covering her ankles.

Without the hair framing her face, all her features stood out, and Taylor stared at the cowlick at her crown, and the shape of her face, and was struck with a single thought.

She is Sam's child.

That was something they'd have to deal with later. She went over and pulled the comforter up and over Alice, all the way to her chin. She felt her forehead, relieved that she seemed cooler. She probably needed sleep more than anything they could give her. Poor kid had dark circles under her eyes, and she was so thin and pale.

Brooke was a horrible mother.

Unless she'd been in an accident or something that prevented her from returning, she was about to be slapped with a child endangerment charge. And anything else Taylor could think up.

When she returned to the other room, Hank and Honor hadn't moved.

"Hi, you little turkeys," Taylor said, getting a little smile from Hank. He was just precious. "Let's see if we can find some pajamas in here somewhere."

She dug around in their dresser until she found something for them to wear. Quickly, she got them dressed and combed out Honor's long hair, braiding it down her back and securing it with an elastic from the bathroom drawer.

Hank waited patiently, sucking his thumb as he clung to a ratty baby blanket from his bed. He looked wide-eyed and a bit in shock, and Taylor wondered what he thought about the last few days and the absence of his mother.

"Come on, you two. Let's go tuck you in on the couch and we'll find a movie for you to watch. Remember Sam, who came in with me? He's bringing you soup and, for dessert, some yummy popsicles. Sound good?"

They both nodded.

She got them both on the couch, found a Disney movie, then —as they settled in—she stroked their heads and tried to soothe their fears, She couldn't help but wonder what had led to this situation, but she didn't have time to linger.

Once they were completely submerged in the fairytale, she got busy. Growing up with three little sisters had taught her to be a fast cleaner-upper and, by the time that another half hour had rolled by, the living room was neat as a pin, and she was on the last of the dirty dishes. She'd cleared the table and the counter tops and had swept the floor.

Sam knocked twice, then opened the door and froze when he looked around. His gaze went from the kids on the couch to Taylor at the sink, disbelief registering in his eyes.

"Who are you and what have you done with Deputy Gray?" he asked.

CHAPTER 11

*T*aylor was on her sixth phone call of the morning. She took a sip of coffee and watched Sam. His back was to her as he stood at the stove, cooking bacon and eggs. He'd put a pan of frozen biscuits in the oven, and the comforting aroma already filled the air. The smell of vomit had gone away, though it had taken her scrubbing the couch and a spot on the carpet with baking soda and white vinegar to knock it out.

This morning she'd moved up to sleep on the couch while Sam went back to the store and got loads of groceries to fill the pantry and refrigerator. Her back was killing her.

"Any updates?" he asked, turning around.

She rarely saw him unshaved, but he pulled off the sexy, roughneck look amazingly. The dish towel he'd tucked into his waistband and the spatula he carried only added to her fantasy and she looked down at her hand, glad to see the ring on her finger. She looked forward to more mornings watching him cook, but hopefully not with sick kids in the next room.

"The sheriff knows the chief of police here. He talked to him and they're sending over someone from child services in a few hours. So far, no news on where Brooke or Derek are, but they've got an APB out for their vehicles. None of the hospitals around here have them admitted, and the local urgent care clinics say they've not seen them either."

Being in law enforcement got her more information than the average citizen, and she'd unapologetically used her credentials in every call.

She and Sam had slept on a pile of blankets on the living room floor, but Taylor had cleared that decision with the sheriff first. Once they'd fed and medicated the little kids, they'd called him, waking him up from an early night to bed. It was awkward, but he'd taken it well and he had a lot of trust in Taylor. If she said the situation needed them to stay there, he was good with that. While catching him up on the situation, she'd said that Sam had just recently found out that Alice is his daughter, and that was why she'd called him.

She hoped that Sheriff didn't catch her stretching the truth.

Technically, they didn't know if she was his daughter.

But, intuitively, she was sure.

Sometime today she had to tell Sam, too. Speaking of the little she-devil, Alice shuffled in and sat down across from her. She rubbed at her eyes, then looked up.

"You're still here," she said, her gaze going from Taylor to Sam.

"Of course we are. We couldn't leave you guys," Sam said, smiling at her.

Alice peered around Taylor, looking into the living room where her siblings sat on the couch, under a blanket, with their eyes glued to the television where cartoons played loudly.

"They look better," she said. "At least they aren't crying."

"They're feeling pretty good today," Taylor said. "Last night I got them to eat a little soup, drink some Pedialyte, and take some fever reducer. Today we must concentrate on lots of fluids. For all of you. How are you feeling?"

Alice yawned. "Embarrassed. I shouldn't have been such a

baby. I was just so tired. I'm sorry that I left you to do everything by yourself. I was only going to lay down for a second."

Sam came over and put his hand on her shoulder.

"Don't say that, Alice. You're twelve years old and you've been doing the job of an adult for days on end. I'm proud of you. Not only for taking care of them, but for calling me when you hit a wall. That was a very mature decision."

Taylor nodded her agreement. "You did the right thing."

Alice blushed. "Thank you for coming. Both of you."

Sam waved his spatula. "Oh, just you wait until you taste my scrambled eggs. I've been practicing."

"Everyone can make scrambled eggs," Alice said, grinning. "I make them all the time."

"Not like mine, you don't. And don't come snooping over my shoulder to see what I do different, either." He turned back to his skillet with an exaggerated huff and Alice giggled.

He was going to make a great dad.

"Alice, now that you're up, I need your help," Taylor said. "Let me make you some juice first. You need to hydrate." She hated to get serious so early, but she needed to get back to work as soon as possible. They had another interview lined up with Larson Swanson later.

Quickly, she poured some apple juice and brought it over and put it in front of Alice. She felt her forehead and was relieved to find it cool.

"Okay, I need you to think hard, Alice. I feel like you must have someone in your family we can call to come over and stay with you until they figure out where your mom is," she said, taking her seat again. With Social Services coming, they needed to figure out something quick before the kids had to go into custody.

"A grandparent maybe?" Sam asked.

Alice shook her head. "My mom doesn't speak to her parents."

"What about your dad's?" Taylor asked.

"Derek's dad is dead, and his mom isn't really like a grandma. Mom hates her. But I guess you could call her."

Taylor had two immediate questions in her mind. First, why hadn't Alice mentioned the grandmother last night when she'd been asked that specific question and, next, why was she calling her dad by his first name? But she kept them to herself and remained patient.

"Do you have her number?"

Alice got up and went to one of the kitchen drawers and pulled it open. She sorted through some clutter, then pulled out a small, tattered notebook.

"It might be in here," she said, bringing it to the table. She flipped through the pages, then pointed at a page. "Right here."

Taylor looked. It read **Dragon Lady**. She suppressed a smile.

"What's her real name?"

"Lois." Alice rolled her eyes to the ceiling and pulled her bathrobe tighter around her.

"Okay. I'm calling her. I'll put her on speaker, but you guys let me do the talking." She looked at Sam specifically. No need to explain why a man was in the home with her grandkids.

Taylor punched the digits into her phone, her heart pounding as it rang several times before a weary voice answered.

"Hello?"

"Is this Lois?"

"Yeah, who's this?"

"My name is Deputy Gray, and I'm here with your grand-daughter. We can't seem to locate their mother. Do you know where she is?"

Taylor could hear Lois exhale loudly.

"Oh, yeah, I know where she is. She's in the psych ward over in the next county."

Raised eyebrows all around, Taylor turned the sound down on her phone a bit so that the little kids couldn't hear from the living room.

"What hospital and how did you get this information?"

"I don't know what hospital. My son told me she'd gone off the deep end again. Begged him to come home and, when he wouldn't, she checked herself in and told them she wanted to kill herself. I'm telling you, that woman is crazy, and she wants to take my son round the bend with her."

Taylor was seething. "If you knew about this, why didn't you come over here and help with the kids?"

"Why would I? Alice takes care of them all the time anyway. She can handle it. I did ask though. Derek said they'd be fine."

"And where is their dad?"

Lois hesitated. "He had to go out of town on business. Someone needs to make the money to pay those bills."

"What sort of business?" Taylor asked.

"What is this? The Spanish Inquisition?" Lois said. "He does construction. Or something like that."

"He's probably at the casino in Cherokee," Alice whispered.

Taylor turned the phone the other way. It wouldn't do to make Lois mad. She was all they had at the moment.

"Listen, Lois. We need someone to come take care of the kids until one of the parents returns. We can't leave them here alone. Alice is a great babysitter but not for days on end. It's not legal."

"Nope. Not me. I have my own life. I can't handle three kids. Especially the oldest one. That one thinks she's smarter than me."

Alice looked at Sam and whispered. "See, I told you she doesn't like me."

Taylor could see the tic in his jaw pumping away.

"I don't want to stay with her anyway," Alice said quietly, almost under her breath.

"Could you at least come get Hank and Honor?" Taylor said to Lois.

"I guess I could do that, but I don't think it's really needed. Alice knows how to take care of them. She's been doing it for a while now."

"I told you," said Alice.

Taylor nodded at Alice to let her know she'd heard, but she needed to deal with Lois first. "Listen, someone from social services is on their way over here. If you don't want Derek's kids to go into temporary foster care, you'd better come get them."

Lois switched subjects. "Did Alice call you? Does she know she's going to be in a lot of trouble when her mother gets home? And if Derek makes it back first, she'd better be ready for the belt."

Taylor exchanged glances with Sam. Leaving Alice behind was not going to be an option for now. She didn't have to say the words. Sam read her mind.

He turned to Alice. "Alice, we're taking you with us. At least until your mom gets back."

Alice's eyes widened. "You really mean it?"

Taylor nodded as she put her hand over the phone. "Temporarily. Until we figure this all out."

"Are you still there?" Lois said.

"We're here. You coming or not?" Taylor asked. She hadn't even met the woman and already disliked the sound of her voice.

"Fine. Give me an hour to get dressed. I'll come stay until Derek gets back. If I bring them here, I'll have to take them to preschool. They can keep catching the bus there—from their house."

Lois didn't wait for a response. Just disconnected the call.

"Alice, set the table," Taylor said. "We have a lot to do, so let's get breakfast out of the way."

"Yes, ma'am. But, you know, Lois is right. I get them ready for school every morning, make sure they're dressed, feed them breakfast, and pack their lunches. Then I walk them to the bus stop. After school, I help them with homework, sometimes even cook dinner, and tuck them into bed." She said it all with a proud chin. "Sometimes they even sleep in my room because they're scared of the fighting between Mom and Derek."

It all sounded very familiar to Taylor, and she was thrust into her past for a moment.

"I'm impressed," Sam said. "But that's a lot for a twelve-year-old. You're incredibly strong, Alice."

"I have to be," she replied, then dropped her voice to a whisper. "I don't have a choice."

CHAPTER 12

*T*he interrogation room in the police department was filled with an air of palpable tension. Shane and Taylor sat across the table from Larson, who looked uneasy in the harsh glare of the overhead lights. Beside him sat his uncle, his expression grim and the knuckles on his folded hands white. Two weeks in and they still didn't have a prime suspect. Taylor hoped that today would grant them a new lead.

First, she had to get her mind in the game. Sam was home with Alice, and, before she'd left, he'd looked at her with an expression of panic and asked her how long she had to work.

She felt sorry for him. He didn't know what to do with a twelve-year-old.

But they had a double murder to solve and, as much as Taylor would love to be there with Sam and help him get to know Alice with less awkwardness, she had a job to do. The Swanson family deserved her undivided attention.

She leaned forward, her eyes on Larson as she began the questioning. "Larson, I know this is difficult, but we need to go over what happened that night one more time. Can you tell us when Abby woke you up and what she said?"

Larson shifted uncomfortably in his chair. "It was sometime after midnight," he began, his voice quivering slightly. "Abby said she saw a man outside. I thought she was just having a bad dream, so I told her to get in bed with me and go to sleep."

Taylor took her turn, her eyes focused on Larson. "And the next morning, when you went downstairs and didn't find your mom in the kitchen, what did you do?"

Larson's eyes dropped to the table, his voice trembling. "I looked out the window, and that's when I saw her ... her body." He swallowed hard. "I called 911."

Shane leaned back, retrieving a piece of paper. "We have the transcript of your 911 call, Larson. The first thing you said was, 'I think my parents are dead.' But you didn't mention seeing your dad dead before you made the call. You said you came down and looked out the window, saw your mother, then immediately called. Can you explain that?"

Larson hesitated, beads of sweat forming on his forehead. He finally spoke, his discomfort evident. "I ... I guess I was just ... I don't know. I was in shock, I think."

"Since the day they came home, Kimberly has taught her kids to call emergency services in any emergency. I taught mine the same. That's what kids do," the uncle said, his tone daring them to question it.

Shane continued, "Well, Larson, who do *you* think could have done this? Any thoughts?"

At first, Larson appeared hesitant, as if battling with his own thoughts. He finally spoke, his voice wavering. "I don't know. A stranger probably. I really don't know."

"You said nothing was missing," Shane reminded him.

"That I know of," Larson said. "But I only got a quick look and haven't been let back in since. Maybe there were things stolen that I didn't see at first."

Taylor doubted it.

"Let's switch gears," Shane said. "Do you know if your mother had any enemies?"

"No. Everyone loved my mom."

"What about at school? Do you know if she had disagreements with any of the staff? Sometimes there can be a lot of drama within the teacher's circles," Taylor said. She didn't know that for a fact, but workplace coworker drama existed everywhere, as far as she was concerned.

"Not really. I mean, sometimes Mom got frustrated about school."

"About what? Can you remember anything specifically?" Shane asked.

He shrugged. "Just the workload. She was always grading papers or having to pitch in after school for events that weren't hers. Oh, and she was always worried that she didn't have a big enough budget for the supplies she needed to teach with. Dad was a penny pincher and she had to ask him before she bought anything. When it was for her classes, he got angry and told her he shouldn't have to pay more for what his taxes were already footing. I think he said something to the principal about it one day when he was there, and Mom got mad at him for embarrassing her."

"What did your dad say to him?" Taylor asked.

His uncle threw his hands in the air. "Oh, for grief's sake. Larson wasn't there. Kimberly told me about it, and it was nothing. Bishop would never make a scene. He'd get his point across, but he'd do it like a gentleman."

Taylor saw a tic moving in Larson's cheek. She wondered if he agreed with that assessment.

But then, as if something nagged at him, his expression changed. His eyes clouded with uncertainty, and he began to speak, his words were slow. "There's something that bothers me," he admitted, his voice breaking. "I remember this one time when my dad was punishing Marc for sneaking the car out. He made him stay out all night. Told him he couldn't come in until he'd removed a stubborn stump from the backyard. I went out there a few times to check on him, and, at one point, he was so mad ... he said he was going to kill our dad. He had the maul in his hands and a strange look in his eyes."

Shane and Taylor exchanged concerned glances. They'd already heard this story once. It must've been a big deal.

"But," Larson continued, tears forming in his eyes, "I don't really think my brother would ever hurt our mom. I didn't mean to say that. I'm just so confused."

His uncle intervened, his voice firm. "That's enough, Larson. If they want to continue questioning you, we need a lawyer."

The mention of a lawyer halted the interview immediately. Shane and Taylor watched as Larson and his uncle left the room, a sense of uncertainty hanging in the air.

Once they were alone again, Taylor turned to Shane.

"Not sure that was beneficial, other than now he's going to lawyer up."

Shane nodded, his expression troubled. "Marc's girlfriend is here. Maybe she has something helpful to say."

They had her waiting in Shane's office so that she wouldn't cross paths with Larson, and Taylor went to get her while Shane headed for a bathroom break.

Penner was in the hall and punched her affectionately on the arm when he went by.

"Hey, Sleuth."

"Hi, Penner. How's it going?"

He shrugged. "Same old stuff. I'm writing up the blotter and have a good one. Mrs. Webster called in last night and wanted someone to go to the liquor store and intervene."

"On what?"

"Her son buying a bottle. Someone from her church called her and said she was going by and saw him getting out of his car in the parking lot."

"That's insane. Isn't her son like ... thirty-seven?"

"Yeah, that's what's so funny. On that note, Grimes arrested a guy for shoplifting from Walmart last night. Get this; Grimes' wife was there shopping and saw a guy stick a package of sheets down the back of his pants. She called Grimes. The thief tried to walk out of the store and right into Grimes' arms. He didn't realize he looked like SpongeBob walking around. Gotta love it," he said.

"She's a pistol, too. Grimes' wife," Taylor said.

"Lydia," Penner said. "Yep, she should've been a cop herself. She keeps Grimes and those two teenage girls on the straight and narrow."

Taylor had been to the Grimes' house a few times. Once for a holiday gathering and another time for Grimes' birthday cook-out. Their home was lively, full of energy and that good feeling of everyone is welcome there. Lydia had made her feel especially comfortable, and Taylor remembered that she'd said she met Grimes during one of their community outreach programs that their department put on. He was giving a talk about the importance of law enforcement and community partnership.

Lydia, being the youngest member of the residents' association and proud of her accomplishment of buying her first home at such a young age, had questions, lots of them, challenging Grimes at every turn. She said instead of being put off, Grimes admired her passion and conviction, and, after the meeting, had asked her out. They were married two months later and immediately started their family. Lydia wasn't a procrastinator. When she had her mind made up, she went full force ahead.

"Maybe we should retire him and put Lydia in his place," Taylor said. "We need another strong woman here to help me deal with all this testosterone."

Penner laughed and started walking away.

"Wait," Taylor said, "Can you pull up some background intel for me?"

"Sure. Whatcha got?"

"Clayton Davis, the principal of the local high school. Background screen, arrests, complaints, anything you can find."

"On it," he said, giving a thumbs up. Then he stopped and turned again. "Oh, I heard you had a chance encounter with our buddy, the disgraced McElroy. He give you any trouble?"

"Nope. Sheriff and Shane were there, so he pretty much pretended I didn't exist, which is the way I prefer it. But thanks."

He gave her another thumbs up and went on his way, whistling the Mayberry tune.

Taylor opened Shane's office door to find Brandy Carrillo's mother looking nervously at her. Brandy sat in the other chair. She was a young brunette in her late teens with a confident posture, a stark contrast to the apprehension that hung in the air.

"I'm Deputy Gray. Please follow me."

They jumped to their feet and fell in behind. Taylor led them into the interview room and beckoned for them to sit at the other side of the table, then she shut the door.

"This is Detective Weaver, the lead on the Swanson case," she said. "Detective, this is Brandy and her mother, Malena Carrillo."

Shane nodded and greeted them. "Thank you both for coming in today. We'd like to hear your perspective on the Swanson family and the events leading up to the tragedy."

Brandy, her eyes somber, nodded and began to speak. "I can't even believe this is happening. I just saw Marc's parents last weekend when I was leaving the center from visiting him. This feels like a movie, or a dream. It's surreal."

"Did anything seem amiss when you ran into them?" Shane asked.

"Not really. No more than the usual awkwardness, but Mr. Swanson and Marc butted heads quite a bit. They had a lot of disagreements, you know? It wasn't easy for Marc."

Shane took a note.

"Did you ever visit Marc at home?" Taylor asked.

Brandy hesitated for a moment before responding. "Yes,

sometimes, but I wasn't comfortable there. And, well, his parents didn't really like me because, first, I'm Mexican, and second, I'm not Catholic."

"Are you saying they were racist?" Shane asked.

Brandy shrugged. "Marc said his dad told him he wasn't going to have a future with *one of them*, meaning someone like me. So, what do you think?"

Malena, Brandy's mother, chimed in, her tone filled with concern. "They were never very welcoming. I wanted to say something about it, but Brandy wouldn't let me. It's so hard for a mother to see her daughter in a situation like that."

Brandy continued, determined. "I did everything I could to make Marc straighten up and do better. I even helped him with his homework when I could. He was starting to do better with his grades. I honestly can't believe he could be involved in something like this."

Taylor's focus shifted to Larson. "What can you tell us about Larson, Brandy?"

Brandy sighed, her gaze distant. "He's nice enough to me but he's not the Golden Boy that everybody thinks he is. Lately, he's been having issues with his dad, too. With Marc out of the house, Larson told me he feels like the newest scapegoat."

The revelation caught Taylor's attention, and she jotted down some notes. It seemed that the Swanson family had been grappling with internal strife with more than just one child.

"He told us he doesn't have a girlfriend. Is that true?" Taylor asked.

"Not right now. He doesn't have anyone exclusive. But he's had them here and there. He's popular with the girls."

"Where were you that night?" Shane asked.

She stopped chomping on her gum and replied without hesitation, "I was at cheerleading practice, and my coach can confirm. My car was in the shop because it needs new brakes, so my mom picked me up afterward."

Malena chimed in, offering her confirmation. "We stopped by Dairy Queen for a milkshake, and then we went straight home. Brandy didn't leave the house again."

"And how do you know that?" Taylor asked.

The mother looked at her daughter and a tense moment passed between them.

"She got caught sneaking out one night and her dad put a keycode on the doors. She has her own code in case of emergencies, but we get a notification of every open and close. He checked it for that night and confirmed that she didn't leave. I can get that to you if needed. Also, her bedroom is on the second floor with no balcony or roof to climb out on. She'd have to jump far enough that she'd break a leg."

Shane nodded and moved forward with the questioning. "Did you speak to Marc that night, Brandy?"

Brandy nodded. "Yes, of course, we talk every night before lights out. Sometimes after, but that night I was tired from practice, and I went to sleep earlier than usual."

Taylor interjected, her tone measured. "We can check records to verify that. It will show which cell towers your phone pinged on. Is there anything you'd like to confess or change in your statement knowing that?"

Brandy's eyes met Taylor's with unwavering determination. "No, I'm telling you the absolute truth. And Marc isn't as bad as people make him out to be. He has a lot of demons from the time he was abandoned and in foster care, but he wouldn't hurt anyone."

Malena spoke up, her voice filled with concern. "Do you need my daughter to take a polygraph test to eliminate her as a suspect?"

Shane considered for a moment before responding, "That won't be necessary at this time, Mrs. Carrillo. We appreciate your cooperation."

"Thank you for your time. We'll call you if we have any more questions," Taylor said. She stood and opened the door. "Can you find your way out?"

"Yes, we're fine," Malena said. "Come on, Brandy. We need to stop and drop off your brother's lunch box he forgot."

When they were gone, Taylor shut the door and sat back down.

"What do you think?" Shane asked.

"Feels like they're telling the truth, at least about Brandy not leaving the house."

"Now what?"

"I want to see if the principal has any kind of past history. Something about him keeps niggling at me so I've put Penner on that. Also, I think we should interview the staff members who were on duty for Marc's floor the night of the murders."

Shane nodded slowly and tapped his pen on the table. It was something he did that irritated her to no end.

"Good idea. Set the facility interviews up for after lunch, please. We can go to them. Check in on Marc again while we're there. Want to go to The Den with me and grab a sandwich?"

"Can't. I need to run by Sam's house for a few minutes. I'll set up the interviews on my way."

"Something going on at home?" he asked, feigning concern.

Taylor didn't believe for a minute he cared about Sam. She wasn't about to tell him about Alice, to give him yet one more reason to feel that Sam wasn't the right one for her.

"Nope," she lied. "Just need to pick up something I forgot."

They locked gazes in a stare down.

"Seems forgetfulness is in the air today," Shane said, then got up and walked out of the room, leaving Taylor sitting at the table. "Have a nice lunch break."

For someone that was over her—and on to the next sister—he sure did get uptight when she mentioned Sam.

CHAPTER 13

*S*am leaned in under the open hood of the weathered sedan, his hands navigating the familiar landscape of its engine. He was relieved to be done with the Mini Cooper, but his back wasn't yet quite recovered from the game of Twister it took to complete the repairs.

The midday sun bore down on him, casting a shimmering heat haze over the asphalt of his driveway. He squinted against the brightness, every now and then glancing toward the lawn chair where Alice had settled with her book, not thirty feet from him. A spot she chose on her own, even when he suggested she might be more comfortable inside or on the porch swing. At twelve, she was in the awkward, gangly stage but, somehow, she'd made herself comfortable with her long legs tucked in around her in what looked like an impossible yoga position.

The title of her book was *Jane Eyre*, and he'd never heard of it, nor would he attempt to ever read a book that looked heavier than the average water pump he put on a car. However, its thickness of pages seemed to have brought her more joy than the title, which proved girls were weird.

The library trip earlier that morning had been an eye-opener.

She'd stocked up on a stack of books that rivaled the height of her slender frame. Her love for reading had taken him by surprise in a world where most her age couldn't get their nose out of their phones, and he couldn't help but feel a surge of respect for the bright, mature young girl sitting just a few feet away. The first thing he'd had her do that morning was send an email to her teachers, asking for assignments to keep up with school until she got back. She'd told them it was a family situation and that someone would call the school later.

Sam would ask Taylor about that. He didn't want Alice to be in trouble because of their decision to bring her home with them.

Alice, lost in her novel, suddenly stirred. With a graceful stretch, she extended her arms high above her head, her fingers grazing the clear, blue sky. A mischievous grin danced across her lips as she glanced down at Diesel, who had brought a tattered ball and dropped it at her feet. She scooped it up, her laughter filling the air as she hurled it across the yard, the dog darting off in pursuit.

Sam continued his work, periodically sneaking glances in her direction. She was a remarkable kid, he thought, her spirit resilient in the face of the chaotic circumstances that had brought her into his life.

As the minutes passed, Alice approached him, her curiosity evident in the quirk of her brow. She leaned against the car, peeking under the hood.

"What are you doing, Sam?"

Sam looked up, wiping his grease-smeared hands on a rag. His eyes met hers, and, for a moment, he was struck by the dimple that deepened in her cheek as she smiled. It was the same dimple he saw in the mirror every day.

"Just some minor repair work on this old girl." He loved working on older cars. So much simpler than dealing with all the new electronics and hard-to-find parts that new cars needed.

Alice perched herself on the fender, her feet swinging just above the ground.

"I can't wait to get my driving license and have my own car."

The prospect of Alice getting her license made Sam nervous. "Well, you've got a bit of time before that can happen."

"I can have my learner's permit in two and a half years," she said confidently.

"That's great," Sam said, though it felt like kids got to get behind the wheel younger and younger, and it was a scary thought to imagine Alice driving. He returned his attention to the motor and using the hood of the car to hide under. An awkward silence hung in the air, heavy with unspoken questions and emotions.

"I want a Tesla," Alice said. "Solid Black. I'll call her Shadow."

Sam chuckled.

"Well, that might be possible once you graduate school and find a great job, but you might have to start with something cheaper to begin with. And your first car should be something safe. Like a Honda Civic."

"No ... that's boring."

"But it's a solid choice. Trust me," Sam said, then cursed under his breath when he dropped his wrench and it went straight through to the ground.

"I'll get it." Alice crouched down and reached for the tool, then handed it up to him. "I know what we can do," she said, "You could show me some things I'll need to know about cars."

Sam smiled from under the hood. He wasn't so thickheaded that he didn't know what she was doing. He'd been around the female species long enough to recognize when one wanted his attention and wasn't going to give up until she got it.

His expression softened as he nodded. "Sure thing. Let's start with the basics." He walked her through the essentials—checking the oil, the water levels, and other routine maintenance tasks. He let her pull out the dipstick and wipe it down with the clean rag from his back pocket, then taught her how to read it. She wasn't even concerned about getting her hands dirty, and that made him proud.

"If you learn to maintain your vehicle, you'll save a lot of money later down the road on repairs. I can't tell you how many motors I've rebuilt because someone was too lazy for scheduled maintenance and let their cars run out of oil until they just quit."

"Mama takes her car to Jiffy Lube for the oil. But I want to be self-sufficient."

He laughed. "That's fine that your mom does that. Some people don't want to deal with getting dirty. But that's costly, too. She should get your dad to do it. Will save them a lot of money."

Alice frowned. "He's not my dad."

Sam stopped. It looked like he wasn't going to be able to dodge this conversation. "Let's go inside and sit down. I need some water."

Alice and Diesel followed him into the house and Sam poured two glasses of ice water and brought them to the table. He sat down, then looked at the clock and realized he hadn't fed her lunch yet and had no idea what to make.

"Okay, so tell me. Why do you say that Derek isn't your dad? Your mom said he is."

"Yeah, well she lied." She lifted her chin proudly.

"How do you know that?" Sam gave her the respect of being totally serious with her and not pushing aside her opinion. She was too mature to treat like a child.

"Because I heard it from his own mouth. Last year when he and my mom were in an argument about money. I was in bed, but I could hear them through my wall. He told her he didn't think it was right that he had to support someone else's kid, and that she needed to ask my real dad for child support so they could get out of debt."

"And what did your mom say to that?"

"She told him to shut up before he woke the kids, and that if I ever heard him say that it would break my heart. But she's wrong. It didn't break my heart. I just felt relieved. I knew he didn't like me, but I never knew why until then. And I'm glad he's not my dad because he's a real asshole. Sorry for my language."

"Alice," Sam said, his tone warning even while he suppressed the urge to smile.

"I said sorry. Anyway, that's when I started snooping around to try to figure out who my real dad was. And I found that letter. Then I found you." She laughed, her voice ringing like music in his ears. Her dimple made an appearance once more, and, as Sam watched her, he couldn't help but feel a strange connection—a shared trait that went beyond mere chance.

Could he really be her father?

As he contemplated this, a whirlwind of emotions churned within him. He knew he needed to confront the possibility that Alice might be his daughter, but the weight of the revelation hung heavy in the air. Sam was caught in a whirlwind of uncertainty, unable to define what he felt in that moment. Thankfully he was rescued from responding by Diesel jumping to his feet and giving a short bark.

It was his "Mama's home" bark.

Sam stood and looked out the window. Diesel was right. Taylor was pulling into the driveway. He'd never been so relieved to see her, and he thanked the stars that she'd chosen that instant to interrupt.

"Taylor's here," he said. "Let's go see what's up."

He met Taylor on the porch, and she walked straight into his arms and gave him a peck on the cheek. Just that little bit of contact sent butterflies through him. When she pulled away, he saw she had a box of Bojangles and was so relieved he didn't have to figure out lunch that he felt like he could drop and kiss her feet.

"You two are cute," Alice said, crossing her arms over her chest as she eased into the porch swing.

Taylor laughed. "Just thought I'd stop by and see how things are going. Bring some lunch. What have you guys been up to? I ate a piece of chicken on the way over because I can't stay long. The rest is all yours. Biscuits in there, too."

"Thanks." Sam said.

She handed the box to him, and he set it on his lap. "We'll go in and eat when you leave," he said. "Alice, you want to tell her what we've been up to?"

She nodded happily.

"Sam took me to the library, and then we stopped at Common Grounds. They have great smoothies. I had the mango and Sam had the green one. He's been showing me how to maintain a car, too. I want him to teach me to drive. I wanted a Tesla, but Sam said I need a safer car first and he's probably right. Maybe a Honda. Wait—I thought that was a motorcycle? I can check the oil on your truck if you want me to, Taylor."

She went on so fast that Sam's head was spinning. She was much more talkative than she'd been at her own home.

He met Taylor's gaze, and she raised her eyebrows, an amused look on her face.

"Alice, we can't plan something like that," he said. He didn't want to mislead her.

"Like what? Checking her oil?" Alice said.

"No. Teaching you to drive. Anything can happen in two years from now. You might be on better terms with your dad by then."

She stopped the porch swing with her feet and instantly looked deflated.

"I don't want to go back there," she said.

Taylor went to her and sat down on the swing beside her and put her arm around her shoulders.

"Alice, you probably don't know this, but I grew up in a dysfunctional home, too. Maybe even worse than yours. My mom wasn't there, and my dad had a drinking problem, so sometimes my sisters and I were put in foster care for short periods, and other times for months at a time. Then I grew up and became a sheriff's deputy and I've worked a lot of cases with children involved."

"Okay?" Alice said, her expression puzzled.

"I'm telling you all this because I know how things work with family services and the court system. Unless your parents can be proved unfit, when they are back in the home, you'll have to return. My colleague, Wesley, who has worked in Family Services here in Hart County for years, made that deal with them. And that's just the way it is. Minors can't choose where they want to live or who they want to be with. The courts must make the decision."

Alice looked away, her attention on the lake behind the line of trees.

When she spoke again, she didn't look at them. "They don't care about me though. To Mom, I'm just a babysitter and a housekeeper. To Derek, I'm nothing. Less than nothing. Sam listens to me. Like, really listens. And he cares about my feelings."

Sam's heart lurched. The sorrow he saw in her face was deeper than any he'd ever seen in anyone, and he couldn't understand how Brooke and Derek could let such an amazing kid feel the way they'd made her feel.

What was he missing? Was she secretly a little demon? Manipulative and bratty?

He just didn't see it. And he had no idea what to say.

"I used to think that about my dad, too," Taylor said, saving him. "I took care of my little sisters all the time, just like you do with your sister and brother. But my dad had demons that I didn't understand until years later. He was holding a lot of guilt over a situation with my mother, and my baby brother who died in a fire. It ate at him until he kept trying to numb the pain with alcohol. Your mom loves you, Alice. I'd be willing to guarantee it. But maybe something is eating at her, too. Something that overrides her maternal instinct and makes her selfish and self-centered. You may not understand it now, and I'm not making excuses for her. I'm really not. She needs to be held accountable for neglecting all of you. I'm just saying that, in this life, sometimes we must give grace even when we don't know what it's for. Not for them, but for you and your own peace of mind. It takes a lot more energy to hold a grudge than it does to just let it go."

Alice thought for a minute, then sighed.

"You make a lot of good points, Taylor, and I'm not saying I disagree. I will think over what you said." With that, she got up and went inside, letting the screen door shut gently behind her.

"Wow. She's something," Sam said, once he saw she was out of earshot. "That was a grownup response."

"Reminds me of myself at that age. So serious and mature. Too mature, but I'm not surprised. I found that most kids grow up real fast when they are so responsible for bringing up siblings. Her parents treat her like an adult so that's what she's going to act like."

"Yeah, that bothers me. I mean, it's great to pitch in as a family unit. I think it was better in the old days when brothers and sisters helped take care of each other, but I think they might overuse Alice. There's more going on there than we know, if you ask me."

"I know what you're saying, but, pivoting subjects, Sam, are you seeing what I'm seeing?" She gave him a sympathetic smile.

"What do you mean?"

"Alice is yours. I have not a doubt in my mind. She looks just like you and she even has some of your mannerisms. I watched her walk across the yard last night and she has your walk, in addition to your dimple and your hairline."

He sighed and ran his hand through his hair, not caring that he was still greasy. He couldn't pretend any more. Or hope that it was his imagination.

"Yeah, I see it. But Brooke says she isn't, so there's some reason she doesn't want me involved. And, to tell the truth, it's only taken me one day to realize that I'm not ready to be a dad. It's a lot of work. I'm so invested in how she feels that it's exhausting. I don't want to make her situation worse. Or screw her up."

Taylor chuckled. "First of all, that's the kind of thing that will make you a great dad, and, second, you might not have a choice in the matter. I don't think that Alice is going to let this go. You may have to talk to Brooke about next steps."

"Like what kind of steps?" He glanced inside, making sure Alice hadn't come back into the kitchen within hearing range.

She shrugged. "I don't know. Maybe regular visitation?"

"Taylor, you didn't hear her when she called me. I promise you; she will never concede that Derek isn't Alice's father. Brooke is one of the most stubborn human beings I've ever met and, to be honest, she kind of scares me. I don't really want to have her as an enemy."

"Yeah, well, she may have passed that stubborn gene on to her daughter. All I'm saying is, get ready, because I don't think this is going to end simply with Brooke coming and gathering all her children beneath her and going back to the way it was. I believe she's going to see a new side of Alice when she gets home. Just think on that."

CHAPTER 14

*T*aylor and Shane were just pulling into the behavioral health facility parking lot when Taylor's phone rang, and Penner's name showed on the screen.

"It's probably about the principal," she said, debating whether to answer or not.

"Get it. Put him on speaker so I can hear," Shane said, shutting the ignition off and crossing his arms over the steering wheel as he leaned forward.

"Hi, Penner, what's up?" Taylor answered.

His voice came through with a hint of excitement. "I've got some interesting details on Clayton Davis."

"That was fast. Whatcha got?"

"First off, he graduated from the University of Georgia with a bachelor's degree in education, which is the minimum required by the state Then he went on and got his master's degree in educational leadership from Northwestern University in Illinois. He seems to be well-qualified for his position."

"That's it?" Shane mouthed to her, throwing his hands in the air impatiently.

She waved him off.

He had no patience and never appreciated how much Penner's investigations did for her.

"Okay, Penner, what about his previous employment before he came to Hart's Ridge?" she asked.

He didn't keep her waiting long. "Well, here's the intriguing part. Clayton Davis resigned from his last position as an assistant principal at an inner-city school in Chicago."

Taylor's interest was piqued. "Any information on why he resigned?"

Penner didn't miss a beat. "My sources tell me it was because of a controversy involving mishandling of funds designated for the school's underprivileged students. It seems there were allegations of financial irregularities and discrepancies in how those funds were used."

Taylor's mind raced as she considered the implications. She looked at Shane and he raised his eyebrows at her.

"That's quite a red flag," he said. "It could indicate a motive, if he was involved in any similar activities here. Penner, see if you can find out any more details and if there were any legal actions taken against him."

"Ten-four."

Taylor thanked Penner and hung up, her thoughts now focused on the possibility that the allegations about Davis had anything to do with their case and if Clayton was hiding more than just his past. Had he and Kimberly had a falling out? Maybe over school events? Kimberly was as square as they come, according to everyone who knew her. What if she found out that her principal wasn't as ethical as she thought he should be?

"Let's knock this out," Shane said, opening his door.

They entered the behavioral health facility, Taylor's mind racing with the new information about Clayton Davis. The sterile environment of the facility contrasted sharply with the weight of the situation they were investigating.

Approaching the reception desk, Taylor took the lead—

showing her badge—and quickly explained their purpose to the receptionist. "We need to speak with the attendants who were on duty the evening of June 16th," she said, her tone conveying the urgency of her request.

The receptionist, a middle-aged woman with a tired expression, nodded and picked up the phone. She dialed a number and spoke briefly before hanging up. "Judith Maloney, our patient advocate, will be down in a moment to assist you," she said, gesturing toward a nearby seating area.

Taylor and Shane sat down, their anxiety brimming between them as they waited for Judith. After a few minutes, she showed up, greeted them politely, and showed them back to the conference room they'd been in before.

Once seated, Taylor wasted no time. "Judith, I know we've talked about this, but we're back to see if there's any possibility that Marc Swanson could have left the facility on the night of June 16th. We've got to make completely sure."

Judith started to roll her eyes to the ceiling, but she composed herself quickly. "I understand the gravity of the situation, but Marc has been through a lot since that night. He's been having nightmares, and I won't allow any further distress for him."

Shane interjected, "We're not here to upset him. We don't even need to see him this time. We just need to gather information. Can we talk to the attendants who were on duty that night?"

Judith sighed and nodded. "Very well, but first let me tell you about another boy on Marc's hall. I'll call him Dylan for the sake of anonymity."

"We really don't have time for stories," Shane said.

"Hear me out, and then I'll let you get back to business. Dylan wasn't in foster care, nor adopted, but his uncle had to take custody of him when he was twelve because his parents couldn't handle him, and the uncle was the only one he listened to. That didn't last long though. After a year of turmoil and multiple altercations that resulted in his loss of work tools due to theft or

Dylan breaking them out of anger, the uncle sent him back. A year later the mom begged the uncle to take him again after he'd been caught stealing his sister's underwear and doing inappropriate things with them. He was also threatening to kill fellow students at school. This time they had a plan. The uncle would get full guardianship of Dylan, then immediately place him here in our behavioral program."

"Sounds like a nice kid," Taylor mumbled.

She held her hand up. "It gets better. As you can imagine, the red tape the uncle took on to get Dylan where he needed to be was cumbersome and it took a while. During that time, Dylan stole everything he could get his hands on and hocked it. Aside from that, he *accidentally*," she used hand quotes in the air, "walked in on his aunt while she was showering, then refused to leave the bathroom, and he pulled a knife on a girl in his cooking class. Not once, but twice. Then, for his grand finale, he tried to poison the whole family on Thanksgiving."

"Was everyone okay?" Shane asked.

"Physically, yes. But he has put a lot of relatives through psychological trauma. After the poisoning, he spent three months in a mental hospital before he was finally admitted here. While here with us, he's attacked other residents and has threatened to kill a few. He refuses to take his medications and they must be forcibly given unless we can negotiate with him that day. I don't usually ever give up on anyone but, if I had to give a forecast of Dylan's future, I'd say he's either bound for long-term prison time or an adult long-term mental institution."

"Why are you telling us all this?" Shane asked.

"Because Marc is not that kid. Sure, he's rebellious and he has a problem with authority. But we're working through that. And I'll be honest, he really has some issues with his father and might possibly even hate him. Many kids do when they're teens, but they eventually come out of that. But Marc isn't a murderer. Even if he was, our facility is secure. If anyone wanted to escape and could do so, it would be Dylan. He's the one intent on vengeance. But I assure you, that hasn't happened."

"Thanks for your insight, and your story," Shane said, his tone dry and bored. "But we have an investigation to complete."

She brisked at him, suddenly stiff in her seat. "Fine. And I'm glad you don't need Marc because I can't allow you to speak to him directly any more without his uncle or a lawyer present. I'll go get the night attendants." She left the room with a flounce.

Shane shook his head. "Everyone thinks they know someone until they realize they don't."

"She could be right," Taylor said. "He might not be our man."

"I agree. But I'm not going to let someone who has no experience in investigations tell me who my prime suspect is or isn't."

He was projecting his irritation on her, so she let it go.

Judith returned shortly with a tall, thin young man named Willis and a busty young woman named Patty. They looked apprehensive as they slowly sunk into their seats, sensing the seriousness of the conversation.

Taylor leaned forward, her gaze fixed on Patty first. She could already sense Patty would be the weakest link. "We don't have to tell you that we're investigating the murder of the parents of one of the patients on your floor. We need your full cooperation to ensure that Marc couldn't have left the facility that night. Can you tell us everything you remember?"

Patty hesitated for a moment before speaking. "I've gone back over it in my head a dozen times. It was a quiet night for the most part. We did our rounds as usual, checking on all the patients. Marc was sleeping when I last checked on him around two in the morning."

"Yeah, and every time I looked in, he was there," Willis said.

Shane probed further. "Did you take your breaks together?"

"No. We take turns so that the hall is always covered," Patty said. Her eyes flickered over to Willis before quickly coming back to Shane.

"Really? Would you swear to that in court?" Taylor asked, picking up on the shift.

Patty looked like a deer in the headlights.

Willis sighed. "Okay, yeah. Sometimes we take our dinner breaks together. No one wants to sit in the break room alone for that long. It's boring."

Judith looked like a puppeteer just pulled her strings, she straightened up so fast. She wrote something down on the legal pad in front of her.

"Sorry, Judith," Patty said to her. "Everyone does it."

"Maybe we need a supervisor in here," Judith said.

"No!" both Patty and Willis exclaimed together.

"Just a few more questions," Taylor said to Judith before directing another question to Willis. "How long was your dinner break that night and was it together?"

"An hour, and, yes, it was together. But no one can walk past the break room without us seeing them," Willis said. "We keep the door open."

"Is there a television in there?" Shane asked.

Patty nodded.

"Do you ever get engrossed in watching something and forget the time?" he continued.

She acted like she was thinking hard, then shook her head, but it didn't look too convincing.

"Willis, did you receive any personal calls during your shift?" Taylor asked.

"I don't know. Maybe. Why?"

"Do you take your calls at the desk, or do you walk outside?"

"At the desk," he said, his tone steely. "Or in the rooms. Wherever I'm at unless I'm otherwise detained and can't pick up the call."

Taylor directed her next question at Patty. "Do any of your family members ever visit you during your night shifts?"

Patty's gaze dropped, and she hesitated once again. "Well, my boyfriend did come by once or twice."

"What about on September 16?"

She twisted a long hair between her fingers and a flush started on her neck and moved up into her cheeks until they were scarlet. "Yeah, I went outside to smoke, and he come up. We sat and talked in his car."

Taylor had a feeling they did a lot more than talk in that car.

Shane pressed further. "What time did this happen?"

Patty looked uneasy. "I don't know. Somewhere between three and four in the morning."

"Willis, were you at the desk or in the hall that entire time she was outside?" Taylor asked.

He nodded. "Unless I slipped into the bathroom for a minute, then probably. I mean, yes."

"And if you're in a room with another patient, would Marc be able to slip by you?" Shane asked.

Neither Willis or Patty answered, and they both looked guilty.

Taylor and Shane exchanged glances, their suspicion growing. "And Patty, when you came back in afterwards," Taylor asked, "did you check on all the patients?"

Patty nodded. "Yes, I did. All of them were accounted for, including Marc."

Shane leaned in, his voice firm. "Patty, be honest with us. Have you ever let a patient out if they promised to be back before morning, and they paid you to look the other way? I know you don't make much as a night attendant. Must be hard to make ends meet."

Patty hesitated for a moment longer, then broke down. "Yes, I have, but it's only been a few times, and they always came back. Marc wasn't one of them, though. I swear."

"And have you two ever covered for each other to leave the facility and go home? Maybe punch their timecard in the morning to make it look like they were here the whole shift? A 'you scratch my back and I scratch yours' kind of thing?" Taylor asked.

Patty looked from her to Shane, then to Judith.

She was wavering.

"Before you answer that," Taylor said. "Have you ever heard of impeding an investigation by lying?"

Shane nodded matter-of-factly. "Obstruction of justice. It's a real charge, Patty."

Patty looked terrified.

Judith was instantly tense, so buttoned up tight you couldn't stick a straight pin up her butt. Taylor willed her to stay that way until Patty answered the question.

"I—well—we have done it a few times. Not that night, though. Sorry, Willis." She grimaced and looked down at the table.

"Damn, Patty. We're in so much trouble. Why can't you keep your mouth shut?" Willis said, falling back in his chair and running his hands through his hair.

"I've got kids. I can't get arrested, Willis," she said, glaring at him. She looked at Taylor.

"Yeah, well what're you going to do about those kids when we get fired, dumbass?" he said, looking like he was ready to strangle her.

The tension in the room was intense as Taylor and Shane processed everything they'd heard. They'd gotten enough out of Patty that they now knew they couldn't trust anything she or Willis said. This was a potential lead; several breaches in the facility's security that might explain how Marc Swanson could have left on that fateful night.

CHAPTER 15

*T*hey say that the fondest memories are made gathered around a table and, with that sentiment, Anna had started a new tradition of Sunday lunches together. She expected everyone to come, and, so far, a few months in they were having good luck in getting the family together.

Taylor was glad to have the day off—or at least part of it— because she would probably go into the department later, and she and Sam had decided to bring Alice to the farm to get her mind off things. A day surrounded by animals and good food could do wonders for a soul.

They approached a small pen housing a handful of rescued goats.

"Meet Bubbles," Taylor said, gesturing to a mischievous troublemaker. "She was abandoned at birth, but we took her in. She's an escape artist and, if there's a way out, she'll find it." She pointed to another one. "And this is Billy, a gentle soul who loves stealing apples from nearby trees."

"I love Billy's beard," Alice said, chuckling.

"He's a rebel," Sam said.

"What do the goats do here?" Alice asked.

Taylor chuckled. "Well, goats weren't part of our rescue plan, but it just kind of happened. Everyone wants goats when they see them as cute little kids, but once they're grown and lose that puppy-like quality and start tearing up things, interest wanes. Hopefully we'll find a farmer soon who will take them and put them to work."

Their tour continued to a small enclosure where a three-legged alpaca named Lucky resided. He was lying on the ground, but they could see where he'd been up and moving around, the hay and dirt disturbed in a five-foot circle around him. That was about as far as he could go.

"Anna is working on finding someone to make Lucky a prosthetic leg," Taylor explained. "He's such a trooper."

"What happened to his leg?"

"He was born that way. The breeder was going to euthanize him, but Jo saw it on the community news page and contacted him. Lucky deserves a chance at life, too."

Alice's eyes sparkled with curiosity as she watched Lucky get up and hobble over to the fence. She put her hand out and he sniffed it.

"Later he'll get some broccoli for a treat," Taylor said.

"Can I give it to him?" Alice asked.

"Of course. You can help with all the afternoon chores if you want," Taylor said.

Sam laughed. "You don't know what you just got yourself into, Alice."

"I don't care," Alice said. "I love animals."

Next, they led her to the rescue dogs' area, introducing her to each one with their unique stories.

"This is Max," Taylor said, pointing to a scruffy terrier mix. "He was found abandoned on the side of the road with a few littermates. The others have been adopted out. Only Max is left."

"And this is Luna," Sam said, pointing at a black cat that had sidled up and was purring against his legs. "She was a stray but she's safe and happy here. She earns her keep, too. She's a heck of a mouser."

They continued, "Meet Perry, a mischievous border collie who never runs out of energy. We're looking for a home for him that includes a job. Borders need to be working or they get ornery," Taylor said.

"What kind of job?" Alice asked.

"Herding, most likely. They were originally bred to herd sheep, but they'll herd anything, even kids."

Alice laughed.

"I'm serious," Taylor said, laughing. "Put a border collie in a yard with a toddler, and it will make sure to keep that kid from leaving the boundaries."

"That's so cool," Alice said,

"Daisy is a senior golden retriever," Taylor said, pointing at a beautiful golden dog that approached them for attention. "She was surrendered by an elderly owner who couldn't care for her anymore."

"Daisy is a dream girl," Sam said, scratching her under the neck. Her tail wagged furiously. "She's going to make some family an amazing dog."

"She's in love with Sam," Taylor told Alice, winking. "But Diesel might not want to share so we have to find her the perfect home."

"I'd never be able to part with any of them," Alice said wistfully.

"Well, we can't keep them all," Taylor said. "That's what rescue is all about. We are a safe place for them to land temporarily, to recover on their way to a better home, handpicked for their specific needs."

"That makes sense," Alice said. "And, with adoption, you get to bring double the happiness. First to the animal, and then to the family who gets them."

"Good point," Sam said.

"And last but not least, Sniff," Taylor said with a smile. "She's a Chihuahua mix with a big personality and an even bigger bark. She was rescued from a pet-hoarding situation."

"What's hoarding?" Alice asked.

"You don't want to know," Sam said. "Let's keep things positive today."

With their tour of the rescue dogs complete, Taylor, Sam, and Alice continued to the separate kennels where dogs were boarded during vacations or business trips.

"We have cozy indoor and outdoor spaces, depending on the dog's needs," Taylor explained. "And each dog has their own little porch with a doggie door to their kennel."

Inside the building, they showed Alice a section for the very small dogs, with its homier atmosphere and indoor play area.

"Sniff spends time in here, too," she said.

"I wish I could have a dog," Alice said, her voice sad. "Honor is allergic."

"What're y'all doing?"

Taylor turned to find Levi, his hands in his pocket as he looked shyly at Alice.

"Levi, this is Alice. She's a friend of ours."

"Hi," Levi said to her, shyer than Taylor had ever seen him act.

"Hey. I like your name," Alice said.

"Want me to take you to see my horse, Apollo?"

Taylor had to smile at that. Apollo wasn't just Levi's horse, but he liked to think he was. To give him credit, he did manage to do most of the care for Apollo. Teague was supposed to help, but he needed a lot more persuasion to get down and dirty around the farm.

"Sure," Alice said.

Levi led the way and Taylor and Sam followed along behind the two kids, accompanied by Diesel and Lucy's dog, Ginger.

When they reached Apollo, Alice was in awe. She followed

Levi, climbing over the fence and going to the horse to stroke his flanks.

"Don't stand behind his back legs," Levi said. "He usually won't kick but you never know."

"He's so pretty," Alice said softly.

"I ride him sometimes," Levi said, his tone boastful.

"Really?" She looked at Sam. "Is he up for adoption?"

"No," Levi said sternly. "He stays here forever."

"Would you like to ride him?" Sam asked. "I can get a saddle."

Taylor could see her hesitation mixed with a yearning to say yes.

"What would Jane Eyre do?" Taylor asked.

"She'd be brave," Alice said. "I'll do it."

Sam went into the small barn and retrieved a saddle, then returned and put it on Apollo. He adjusted it, fixing it to fit the length of Alice's long legs, then hoisted her up.

She was smiling ear to ear as Sam led her around the enclosed pasture. He talked her through how to give commands, then finally let her hold the reins.

Taylor heard running behind her and looked to find Bronwyn and Teague had joined them.

"Who is that?" Bronwyn asked.

"That's Alice," Levi said.

"She's a friend of mine and Sam's," Taylor added.

"Are her parents here?" Teague asked, looking around.

"No, they're away for now. Alice is Sam's houseguest for a bit." She hoped Teague would leave it at that.

"Which of my favorite grandkids would like to go get me a bottle of water," a voice boomed out.

They turned to find Taylor's dad walking up.

"I'll go, Grandpa," Bronwyn said, then took off running for the house.

"Hi, Dad. I didn't know you were coming," Taylor said, pleased to see him.

He was dressed in nice jeans and a shirt she'd never seen. He'd lost some weight and his face no longer appeared to be puffy. Even his eyes looked clearer than she'd ever seen them. Cecil had mentioned he was back in AA, and she could see that it agreed with him.

"Anna called me last night and I promised I would. It's only about the millionth time she's asked me. She was starting to get salty about it."

They laughed. They were all afraid of Anna's ire.

Taylor wanted to tell him how proud she was of him for starting his support group again, but that knowledge was a secret she had to keep, until he decided to tell her himself.

Eventually, Sam helped Alice dismount from Apollo and Levi climbed up next. He was showing off in a canter when they heard Cecil yell from the porch of Anna's house, telling them lunch was ready.

"Come on, Levi," Taylor called out.

They all made their way inside, and Taylor introduced Alice around, referring to her as a new friend, with a tone that warned her sisters not to ask for details.

"Hi, Alice, so glad you came," Lucy said, surprising Taylor when she went to Alice and gave her a warm hug. "Gracious, you're tall," she said to Alice.

When standing together they looked the same height, but Lucy was short.

Petite, she liked to remind everyone.

They all filled their plates with Anna's delicious roast beef and sides. The adults sat down at the table, and the kids found spaces around the living room.

Eldon was the first to dig in. He took a big bite, then closed his eyes and moaned. "Anna, I have no words. You've outdone yourself."

"Eldon!" Jo said teasingly. "Stop flirting with my sister. I told you to pay for cooking classes for me and I'll make you something just as good!"

Laughter filled the room and Anna blushed, quickly changing the subject.

"What're you two working on down at the theatre?" she asked.

"*Little Shop of Horrors*," Eldon said. "Perfect for the upcoming season. Should be ready by Halloween week. You know, Anna, you should come try out. I think we have a part that might be good for you."

"I don't know about that," Jo teased. "Maybe if we needed someone to play the White Witch in *Narnia*."

Everyone laughed, except for Cate, who seemed distant, like she wasn't even listening.

"Why isn't Ellis here?" Taylor asked quietly, leaning in to whisper to Cate.

He usually always came to their family gatherings.

"He's working on clearing some property. He's going to break ground in a few months to build a house."

"Have you seen the property?"

Cate shook her head. "No. He hasn't invited me to."

Taylor saw her dad looking at them, and then look away. His eyes held pity, so he must've heard them. Cate might be facing the end of her relationship with Ellis, whom she had seemed so happy with, and that was sad. She recalled that Ellis' adult children had disapproved of their dad dating her due to her past incarceration and thought what a loss for them not to recognize Cate's true character.

"What about his houseboat?"

"Selling it," Cate said, picking at a potato on her plate. She'd barely touched anything. "Said he's going to buy a ski boat once he's settled into the house."

"Ski boats can be fun," Taylor offered, not knowing what else to say.

Lucy heard them. "I'm selling my boat, too. Time to get our

feet back on the ground permanently. On that note, Taylor, did you decide if you want to keep your cabin or let me have it? I can always pay for it with what I get from the boat."

"That's up to Cate. It was her money that built the cabins. Still don't know if I'm moving out for good." She glanced at Sam, who was in deep conversation with Eldon now. She wasn't sure what was going to transpire with their relationship now that Alice was in the picture. "Can you give me some more time to think on that, Lucy?"

She shrugged. "Yeah. No worries. I can build my own if I need to. Once I sell the boat, I mean. Which shouldn't take long considering how nice Jo helped me make it inside. Sam, I might need you to do a tune-up for me before I list it, though."

Sam gave her a thumbs up.

"Girl, you know I still got my place in town," Cecil said to Lucy. "That cabin I stay in during the week is yours. I'll move out whenever you're ready for it."

"No," both Taylor and Lucy said at the same time.

"We don't want you to go anywhere, Cecil," Taylor said.

She meant it, too. Having Cecil there during the week meant everything to her, because she knew it gave him a new purpose in life now that he had his work on the farm.

"I'm just sayin'," Cecil said. "I know this here is family land, and I'm not family. I can go back to staying in town anytime."

Taylor put her fork down. "Well, I'm just sayin' too, Cecil. You *are* family, so don't ever say that again."

He smiled warmly at her. "Don't go get your feathers all ruffled up now. Go back to eating that lovely food your sister done made you."

"I guess it's a good thing I bought this land so long ago," Jackson said, a smug grin on his face. "It's turned into quite the profitable venture for you all."

Everyone around the table quieted.

For one thing, the farm wasn't profitable yet. The money they were making on dog-boarding barely covered what they spent for the overhead like utilities and taxes, and funds to pay for the rescue work. Donations were starting to come as more people learned about the sanctuary, but it was slow going. They'd spent a lot of money building the cabins, the pens, the small barns, and all the dog runs. All of it Cate's money from the state of Montana, that she'd gladly given.

But profitable? That was a big stretch.

Still, Taylor didn't know what to say without hurting his pride. But Lucy, she didn't care.

"Yeah, Dad," Lucy said. "That *was* a good thing. And it was an even better thing that when it was up for auction for back taxes and defaulting on the mortgage because you were drinking up every penny you had and more, Taylor swooped in and saved it, then worked multiple jobs until she paid off your debt."

His smug smile froze on his face, and he set his fork down, scooted his chair back and got up. "Thank you for the meal, Anna." With that, he quietly went out the door.

Jo threw her napkin down. "Damn, Lucy. Could you have been any crueler?"

Shane looked embarrassed; his eyes trained on his plate.

Eldon and Sam pretended ignorance and kept shoveling food into their mouths.

"Yeah, actually, I could've," Lucy said indignantly. "I forgot to throw in the part about his four daughters bouncing back and forth to foster care, without a parent to look out for them."

Cate hung her head, but you could see a red flush on her neck, creeping upward.

Taylor was mortified. Lucy had shamed their dad in front of everyone. Sam and Eldon, and probably even Shane, just got a good look into the guts of their dysfunctional family dynamic. It was embarrassing. She looked into the living room and caught Alice watching them. She had picked up on the sudden tense vibe and she looked worried.

"That's enough of this talk," Taylor said, her voice strong and firm. "Jo, can you watch your language around the kids? And Lucy, I appreciate you defending my honor about the place, but the past should stay in the past. Dad is trying to be a better man and we don't need to keep rubbing his mistakes in his face."

"Then he needs to acknowledge that you are the one who saved this family," she said angrily. "Saved him, too, if you really want to get down to the details."

"Lucy, it's nice of you to stick up for your sister, but I agree with Taylor," Cecil said. "This family has been a long time in coming together like this and, believe me, you don't want to lose the good that you've built up in the last few years. There's nothing worse than being estranged from your own people. You're probably right about your dad, but, on that note, I'm going to go see if he is still out there."

"Thank you, Cecil," Anna said. "Please tell Daddy we're done with this conversation, and I've got his favorite apple cobbler with ice cream on top. To please come back."

"Yes, ma'am." Cecil said, getting up. He took his plate to the sink, then went outside.

"In other news, Corbin has backed out of doing the concert," Jo said. "He's not ready to face his stage fright, even with Hank at his side."

Taylor sat back in her chair and let out a long sigh. That was more bad news. Without Corbin to bring in the fans, the concert probably wouldn't do much to bring in funds for the rescue. Sam reached for her hand under the table. She took it, and was thankful for him. She was also grateful that they had the farm, and that everyone had come together under one roof, but she wondered how long it would be before something would tear them apart again.

CHAPTER 16

The sheriff was mad and could barely stay in his seat. So far, his temper was pointed at Shane, but Taylor was just waiting for her turn. If they didn't settle him down, the whole department was going to hear him through the thick door.

"You go turning over rocks, you better be ready to face what the hell you find beneath," Sheriff said, pointing his finger in the air. "And you damn well better have a good reason for looking. The high school principal called and chewed my ass up one side and down the other this morning after being told he's under investigation from his higher ups."

Shane remained calm. "Yes, sir. That was us. Turns out that Clayton Davis was let go from his position as principal in Chicago. Sources found that it was for mishandling of funds. That was cause for suspicion and we decided to dig further."

"*Sources*. Don't yank my chain, Weaver. You mean Penner."

"Yep," Shane said.

Sheriff hated when Shane acted all big-city-detective and wouldn't think twice about bringing him back down to small-town-reality.

Taylor cleared her throat. It wasn't fair to let Shane take all the heat and she was starting to feel bad for him. She began cautiously. "We had to explore the possibility that something went on here with Kimberly Swanson and Davis, possibly leading him to have a vendetta against her. She was known to be a pillar of morality, and we thought maybe she stumbled upon something unsavory at the school. I'm the one who called the state comptroller's office and asked a few questions."

Sheriff leaned forward and slammed his hand on the top of his desk.

"You'd better hope they found something on him or he's going to slap a lawsuit on this department for defamation."

Taylor didn't know if they had or not. She'd just arrived to work when the Sheriff bellowed down the hall for both to get to his office. There wasn't time to see if Shane had gotten any calls.

Shane smiled slightly in his usual cocky way. "They sure *did* find something."

Sheriff leaned back in his seat, slightly mollified. Enough to lower his voice. "Start talking."

"First thing they did was find out that if he hadn't resigned from the Chicago school four years ago, he would've been fired. They let him save face and his record by walking away without severance."

"How does that factor into our case?" Sheriff said.

"After Gray made the initial calls, I did a follow-up and made a friend named Sally at the comptroller's office," he said, grinning sideways at Taylor.

"Of course you did," Taylor said. She couldn't help the eye roll that came with her response. It never failed for him to use his charm to do his job.

"Keep talking," Sheriff said.

"Ol' Sally did some digging and, turns out, Davis is back to thinking he can do what he wants to with school funds. Turns out he's either got a teacher's pet or dalliance going on with the school librarian. He doesn't know it yet, but Sally at the comp's office will be getting a raise and probably a promotion for what she's uncovered."

"Stop beating around the bush, Weaver. Spit it out," Sheriff said. "You think I have all day to play games?"

Taylor kicked Shane's foot with her own. He was on thin ice, and both would go under if he didn't stop his bullshit.

He opened his notebook and started reading, then looked up. "Sally found out that the librarian, a cute little number named Nora Jean Wick, is also the operator of concessions at the football and basketball games. Sally ran an audit. For this season, Wick has failed to maintain a daily inventory or turn in all the receipts. According to the audit, sales should've brought in more than sixteen grand, but the librarian has only turned in twelve or so."

"That's hardly something that would warrant murdering someone to keep from being found out," Taylor said, hoping he had more.

And he did.

Shane winked at her. "You're right, partner. But Sally also found out that Wick is on the payroll for two positions. Librarian and the wrestling coach for the girl's division."

"So?" Sheriff asked.

"So, they don't have a separate division for the girls. One team. One coach. And it's not the librarian."

Sheriff went quiet, other than the tapping of his pen against his desk.

"Can't tell me he isn't sleeping with her," Shane said.

"Sounds like we need to go to the school and pay Davis and the happy little librarian a visit," Taylor said. "That is, if we can catch him before he's fired and escorted out of there. Otherwise, we might be interviewing him here after the state presses charges against him."

Shane nodded in agreement.

"It could have nothing to do with the Swanson case, too," Sheriff said. "Don't get too trigger happy."

"Agreed," Taylor said. "But it also could be everything to do with it. Maybe Kimberly found out what was going on and threatened to blow the whistle on whatever she knew. People are murdered for a lot less than outing affairs and embezzling a few grand."

"That's what I'm thinking," Shane said. "I did a little snooping this morning, and guess what? While Clayton Davis is a renowned bachelor all the way, little miss Nora Jean Wick is married and a mother of two. That's going to add some more fuel to the fire if Davis' favoritism becomes public. Small towns don't like marital unfaithfulness, especially among those paid to teach their children good morals and values."

"Get up to the school before Hot Pants Sally turns her report over to her supervisors," Sheriff said. "If they arrest him, he won't give you anything."

"Exactly what I was thinking, Boss," Shane said.

"And don't call me boss," Sheriff said grumpily. "Next time, you come in here and be ready to lay the facts out promptly. I'm not interested in an Easter egg hunt every time I talk to you."

"Yes, sir." Shane slapped his notebook shut and stood. He held the door for Taylor.

"I'll be there in a minute," she said. "I need to talk to the sheriff alone for a minute."

She ignored the questioning look Shane gave her before he softly shut the door, and she got down to the point.

"I need Sunday off, Sheriff." She usually had Sundays anyway, but not when they were working a big case.

"Are you *crazy*?" he replied.

She laughed slightly. "Don't ask what you don't want to know. But really, it's important. I have a good lead on my own case." He never had to ask *what* case when she mentioned it. Something about the tone of her voice immediately told him it was about her attack.

"How good of a lead?" he asked instead.

"Very good. We've narrowed it down to four male suspects. All brothers. I got in touch with a DNA expert who used the tip of the fourth cousin to build a family tree, then work from there. She called yesterday and said she now knows who the mother of the four males is and said she lives in Mercer County, West Virginia. With a bit of investigation on social network last night, I found where the woman will be tomorrow. I want to go talk to her."

"Just going to walk right up and tell her one of her sons is a rapist, huh? That should go over well." Sheriff scoffed.

Taylor sighed. She wasn't in the mood for sarcasm.

"No. I'm going in undercover. She won't know why I'm there."

He stared at her, and she could see him chewing at the inside of his jaw.

"I understand if you can't let me go," she said, breaking the silence. "I'll just do it later in the week, when Shane can spare me."

"No, I want you to go. Taylor, do you know why I've never promoted you?"

She shook her head.

"Listen to me. You weren't ready until the last few years, and, now that you have the skills, your job doesn't have your full attention."

"That's not true, Sheriff. You can't say that. You know I'm fully committed to my work and always have been."

He held his hand up. "I can say it and I am. Until you figure out who the son of a bitch is that broke into your home and shattered your sense of security, and—worse—your pride, you'll never be totally committed to the cases you work. In the back of your mind, and sometimes in the front, you are thinking about him. Investigating, even when you aren't. I want you to solve this case and I also want to bring Weaver in on it. Get it done already."

Taylor shot to her feet. "No. Absolutely not. You promised me. Only you and me."

"Sit your ass down." He pointed to the chair. "And you won't use that tone with me ever again or I'll have your badge."

She sat down, gingerly. She could feel the heat of her temper rising through her. Or maybe it was the shame. They were now one and the same when it came to what happened to her. Letting others in on it was something she just wasn't ready to do. It was humiliating enough to tell Sam.

"What's the next steps after you talk to this woman? You plan on breaking down her door and obtaining DNA from all four sons? You know you'll need a warrant for that. We must start doing things by the book, Taylor. This isn't an old western where you can track him down on your own and hang him from a big oak tree. If you aren't careful, you won't be able to use a damn bit of evidence to bring him to justice."

He was right. And that made it worse.

"Just let me talk to her first," she said finally. "I'll be careful."

He nodded slowly. "You go ahead and take Sunday. I'll give you that but don't do anything else until you report back to me. I've given you way too much leeway in this because you know I'm fond of you. But, from now on, we discuss things each step of the way. You understand me, Deputy?"

"Yes, sir." Taylor rose from her chair and took a deep breath and dropped her shoulders before opening the door. She didn't want Shane asking her why she was riled up. "I hear you loud and clear."

TAYLOR LED Nora Wick into the small conference room adjacent to the school library. Shane was behind closed doors in the principal's office with Davis, their planned strategy in place to separate the two and question them before they could concoct matching answers.

Her heart pounded with anticipation. She had to do this right, or Nora would clam up and not say a word. Then Shane would think he had to take a crack at her and get done what Taylor couldn't. She had to prove to the sheriff that she was good at her job.

Nora took a seat across from Taylor, her eyes darting nervously around the room. She was cute, in a teacherly kind of way. She wore her strawberry-colored hair in layers that fell over her shoulders, and Taylor didn't fancy herself very knowledgeable about makeup, but Nora seemed a little heavy on the red lipstick that clashed with her hair. She was dressed in a denim one-piece dress and had a lot of knee showing. With it she wore white sneakers. No socks.

Taylor thought back to when she and her sisters were in school, and how Lucy had been sent home plenty of times for showing that much leg. Things must've changed. Or Nora's ruler was broken.

"Thank you for meeting with me," Taylor said. She planned to stay calm and easygoing. She didn't want to scare the woman right out of the gate.

Wick tried to appear composed, but Taylor could hear a barely perceptible tremor in her voice as she spoke, "I don't know why I'm here. I haven't done anything wrong."

"Didn't say you have, Mrs. Wick. To the contrary, I saw your photo on the school Facebook page today. Looked like you are doing a fine job as the librarian." Taylor had looked Nora up on the way over. She liked to get a sense of who she'd be interviewing.

"Media Specialist. You can call me Nora. And that was me showing a copy of a book donated to us by the Women's Committee through the Farmer's Federation. The committee chair, Meaghan Smith, was in it, too. They're promoting literacy this month."

Taylor nodded appreciatively.

"I've always had a fondness for the librarians," she said. "I think they are much more vital to the growth of a child's mind than people give them credit for."

"Thank you," Nora said nervously. "But that's not what you're here for, is it?"

Taylor fixed her gaze on Nora, her expression unwavering. "No, Nora, it isn't. But the first thing I want to tell you is that it's in your best interest to be honest with me in everything you say."

Nora hesitated for a moment. "Of course. You're law enforcement. What do you want to know?"

"Let's start with Principal Davis. Are you involved with him romantically?"

Nora's cheeks flushed with embarrassment, and she looked down at her hands. "Absolutely not. I'm happily married."

"Well, that was fast," Taylor said. "Already a lie with the first question. You must not care about your children if you are so easy to lie to an official."

"I'm not lying!"

"Will you take a lie detector test?"

Not that they really cared if she was sleeping with the principal or not, but the lie detector test always worked on the non-hardened criminals.

Nora's eyes welled up with tears, and she blinked them away. "Fine. Yes, Clayton and I had a little thing. I was lonely and stupid for a while. I wish I could take it back. Please, you can't tell my husband."

"Did Kimberly Swanson know about it?"

"Kimberly?" she looked confused. "No, she didn't know. Nobody knew."

"Nora, rumors are circulating, and we need to know the truth.

I'm going to ask you again. Did Kimberly Swanson know about your relationship with Davis?"

"I said no. I wasn't really friends with Kimberly. Even if I was, I wouldn't tell anyone about Clayton. The thing about working in a school is one whisper at the morning bell leads to an echo through the halls by the afternoon."

"I don't get it," Taylor said.

"Means if you don't want something talked about, you don't share it with anyone. Not even your teacher best friends. This place feeds on drama—and not only with the students."

"Let me ask you this, Nora. What will your husband say if he finds out that number one, you're having an affair with your boss, and number two, you might be an accessory to a murder."

"What are you talking about? I've got nothing to do with Kimberly Swanson's death," Nora said, her eyes now wide with fear.

"Then you need to start talking." Taylor softened her approach, her voice filled with empathy. "We are trying to understand what happened to Kimberly and her husband. Her family needs closure, Nora. If you cooperate, it may help clear your name. This doesn't have to get back to your husband."

Nora wiped away a tear and sniffed loudly. "I don't know what to tell you. Kimberly was always nice to me and it's tragic what happened to her. If I knew anything about it, I'd be the first to tell you."

"Maybe Clayton told you that Kimberly did find out about the affair. That she threatened to expose it? Now is the time to talk, before you get in over your head."

"No." Nora said, shaking her head emphatically. "He did *not* tell me that. We were careful. No one knows."

Someone always knows.

Taylor wanted to tell her that, but there was still more to get her to cop to. She decided to change tactics. "Tell me about the girl's wrestling team."

Nora squirmed in her chair. Then she got up and retrieved a tissue from a box on the credenza and came back and dabbed the corner of her eyes before speaking again. She was shaking. She knew she was caught on this one.

"Clayton promised me that the money I was getting for being the wrestling coach was just extra funds that wouldn't be used for anything else. He said I might as well take it before the state absorbed it back. I told him it probably wasn't right to do, and I offered to do some clerical work for the team. He was supposed to let me know what I could do. He said he'd talk to the coach."

Taylor raised an eyebrow. "You thought it wasn't right, but you did it anyway and now you're trying to make it sound legit. Why would they pay you for a position that doesn't exist?"

Nora's face contorted with worry. "I just didn't think it was a big deal. Clayton said it was just a formality, and I really thought I'd be helping in other ways eventually."

"Oh? Like skimming funds off the top of the concessions sales for the school events?"

Nora sat upright in her chair. "Now, I did not *do* that. I swear."

"Someone did."

"I turned the funds in to Clayton the morning after each game. Every penny of it."

Taylor couldn't help but feel a pang of sympathy for Nora. It seemed like she had been manipulated by Clayton Davis. "Nora, if not the affair, then we suspect that Kimberly may have discovered something about irregularities in the school funds. Did she confront either you or Clayton about it?"

Nora shook her head vehemently. "Not me, she didn't. I don't steal. If those funds were taken, it was after I'd turned them in."

"What about the receipts, or a daily inventory? There seems to be some gaps in the paper trail of incoming sales vs. inventory."

"I turned those in, too. Just like I was supposed to. Deputy Gray, If I thought being paid as the wrestling coach was stealing money, I wouldn't have done it. Oh my God. Am I going to jail for that?"

She looked like she was on the edge of hysteria.

"I can't speak to that," Taylor said. "It depends on if the state wants to press charges."

Nora was in tears again. "I'm so sorry. I can give the money back. I'm not a criminal. And I'm surely not a murderer. Or an accessory to one. I'll swear that on my children's lives."

Taylor believed Nora's words, and a sense of unease settled in her stomach. "Nora, we need to find out what really happened to Kimberly. If you're telling the truth, it might not be your fault, but Clayton Davis might be involved in something much bigger. We'll do our best to protect you, but you must help us and, if you try to protect him, you'll go down, too."

Nora nodded, her shoulders slumping in relief. "I'll do whatever I can to help. I just want this nightmare to end."

As Taylor left the room to confer with Shane, she wondered if they could possibly wire Nora and let her have a conversation with Davis. Bring up Kimberly and the tragedy. But that depended on how Shane's interview with him went. Something told her that Davis was too smart to run off at the mouth. He probably had his own attorney on speed dial.

CHAPTER 17

aylor stared out the window. Route 52 toward Bramwell, West Virginia, was awash with scenery that transformed into a picturesque landscape of rolling hills and lush woodlands. The vibrant greenery of summer blanketed the region, creating a soothing and inviting atmosphere. Or at least it would if they were there for any other reason than to investigate the crime against her.

Sam drove, while Taylor navigated and Alice sat in the backseat, her nose buried in her schoolbooks and ear pods in, listening to her own music. Sam had loaned her an old phone and set it up with a playlist. She was supposed to have stayed at the farm, but at the last minute she'd felt too shy, and Sam had let her come once she agreed to finish all her homework. She was still logging on every morning to her junior high school portal and, for now, was keeping up.

"*I shot the sheriff,*" Alice sang out. "*But I did not shoot the deputy …*"

Sam laughed at her choice of music.

Taylor wished she could laugh. Not today. Things were

getting complicated on both cases and not being closer to solving one or the other had her nerves in an uproar. If she and Shane didn't nail something down for the Swansons, the sheriff was going to have to call in the state police, and no one wanted that.

As expected, Principal Davis had lawyered up. He was furious that he'd been caught with his hand in the cookie jar, as well as the other incidents, and wasn't saying a word. He'd been put on paid leave pending the investigation from the state. There was sufficient evidence for everything other than anything to connect him to the murders of the Swansons.

"We're getting close," Sam said. He gripped the steering wheel, glanced at Taylor, his face etched with determination.

Taylor nodded; her gaze fixed on the passing scenery. "I can't believe you've gotten us this far," she replied. "Let's hope we can find some answers."

"Wasn't me," Sam said. He lowered his voice in case Alice could hear. "Kathie is as good as people say. She's the one who found the four brothers, and then their mother. All we have to do is narrow it down to which one is our man. I think if we can get the mother to talk about her sons, it will give us a clue who to start with first. Every family has that one troublemaker. He's going to be our guy, I'd bet it."

Taylor was thinking. She didn't want to take the investigation away from Sam. He was trying so hard to help her figure it all out. If she was acting alone, she would probably follow each of the male suspects and grab their DNA via a discarded water bottle, or cigarette. Or whatever she could get her hands on. But running forensics on all four would be expensive and time-consuming. He was right that if they could narrow it down, at least by two of them, they might get to the truth faster.

Alice pulled her ear pods out. She couldn't contain her excitement. "I can't wait to see those big mansions, Taylor! Are they really owned by millionaires?"

Taylor smiled at her. "The houses aren't like millionaires'

homes today. They were owned by millionaires a long time ago and, back then, their size was considered a mansion. They'd be dwarfed by real mansions today, but they're part of Bramwell's history."

They'd agreed that, as far as Alice was concerned, she thought they were just taking a day trip for sightseeing. She didn't need to know the real reason they were there.

"Do you have the address of the first house?" Sam asked.

"Yes, it's right there on the hill," Taylor said, comparing her phone to the numbers on the street sign.

Sam pulled in and drove up the long driveway. They parked and got out and joined the group of visitors gathered outside. The house was the Colonel Thomas House and was built with a Tudor-style architecture. It stood atop a knoll overlooking the town of Bramwell.

Blanche Wagner, their tour guide, greeted them with a warm smile.

She began, "Welcome to the Colonel Thomas House, built by W. H. Thomas between 1909 and 1912. This was the most expensive home in Bramwell, costing a whopping $95,000 back then! This is only *one* of the selection of homes belonging to coal barons who made their fortunes here around our town."

Taylor exchanged a knowing glance with Sam.

Blanche was their girl.

Well, their woman. She was probably in her late sixties or even early seventies. A very well put together woman who reeked of old money.

Taylor wondered why she was working but figured it was part of some sort of charitable work with the local historical society. It was always made up of women like Blanche who had too much time on their hands. Not that it was a bad thing. Taylor wished that she had time for passionate pursuits herself. Maybe someday.

Blanche continued, "The house features a magnificent ballroom on the third floor, where the Thomas family undoubtedly hosted grand gatherings where many debutantes met their husbands." She talked of dancing cards and past traditions, and Taylor could see that Alice was mesmerized by the old stories.

"Many of these homes have fascinating workmanship, including intricate woodwork, stained-glass windows, and stones imported all the way from Europe. Back then, that was quite a luxury because it had to come on a slow ship, and only the wealthiest could afford it."

After they were done with the Thomas House, they toured the Collins House, a beautiful yellow residence with a garden. Blanche shared, "Mr. Collins, a coal operator in the Pocahontas Mine, built this house. He also had a mansion in the heart of Bramwell, the Jairus Collins House." As they moved on to explore more of Millionaire Row, Blanche shared tales of the town's coal mining history and the grandeur that had once been the norm.

After the tour, they all gathered on the street and Blanche wished them well. "If you haven't gotten your fill of coal country history, be sure to visit the restored Bramwell railroad depot. It's an interpretive center and museum for West Virginia's Coal Heritage Trail."

Sam took Alice and pointed out something down the street, just as planned. Taylor waited until the rest of the group had left, then, just before Blanche got ready to walk away, she approached her.

"Blanche, you did such a wonderful job," she said, oozing compliments.

"Why, thank you," Blanche said, looking suddenly modest. "I only recently took this position and I had to do a lot of studying about the history, but it's a fun way to spend my time."

"Speaking of that, my name is Georgia Grayson and I'm a journalist for Timeless Town Times and I'm writing an article about Bramwell that will publish next month. I'd love to pick your brain for more details if you'd be willing."

Blanche paused.

"I could treat you to lunch while we talk. Say, the Vault? Of course, I'd highlight you in the article for the generous time you give toward the historical integrity of the town."

That got her attention and Blanche raised her eyebrows.

Hopefully as planned, she'd take the bait. It was going to be a pricey lunch, but worth it if they got any clues about Blanche's sons.

Blanche touched her hair, patting it into place as she raised her chin. "The Vault is a nice place for a short meeting. Let me just have a few minutes to move some things around on my schedule. I'll see if I can make it work."

She pulled her extra-large smartphone from her bag.

"Great. I'll just go talk to my fiancé while you're doing that," Taylor said. She walked down the sidewalk to Sam and Alice.

"I'm going to go on with Blanche. Sam, you and Alice go somewhere fun for lunch."

Alice looked confused.

"Why aren't we staying together?"

"I have a few other questions for Blanche," Taylor said. "You two have fun and meet me back here in an hour."

"Sounds good," Sam said. "C'mon, Alice. After lunch, we'll hit the ice cream shop."

When Taylor walked back to Blanche, she was ready.

"Do you just want to meet there?" she asked.

Whoops. Taylor hadn't thought that through. "Oh, sure. I can just taxi over. My fiancé already left. He's picking me back up here in an hour."

Blanche seemed to hesitate, then threw her hand in the air nonchalantly. "Well, in that case, I guess you can ride with me. It's just good to be cautious these days, you know."

"Absolutely," Taylor said. "But this way you can tell me more about the town as you drive. If you don't mind, I mean."

"Don't mind at all," Blanche said. "That's my car over there."

She pointed at a cream-colored Mercedes sedan in the lot across from them, then led the way.

⁂

THE RESTAURANT that Taylor had picked was in Bluefield, but only sixteen minutes away. Blanche talked nonstop on the way, only taking a breath when she pulled into the parking lot.

"You're lucky it's a Sunday," Blanche said. "That's the only day they keep lunch hours. Usually, they don't open until five."

Inside was impressive. Very tastefully decorated with an upscale ambiance, and immediately a man approached them and gave Blanche a hug and kiss on the cheek.

"So good to see you, Blanche," he murmured, then stepped back.

"And you, as well, Tony. This is my new friend, Georgia. She's a journalist and is interviewing me for a piece that will run soon. Can you sit us somewhere more private?"

"Of course," Tony nodded and led them down the hall.

"He's the manager and he always gives me and my family personal attention," Blanche whispered proudly.

They settled into a table at the far side of the dining room, and Taylor followed suit with ordering French onion soup and a berry salad. She didn't particularly like fruit in her salad but today was all about stroking Blanche's ego, and imitation was the best compliment.

The only thing she didn't copy was the sangria to drink.

"Are you sure?" Blanche asked. "If you've never had their Perfect Peach sangria, you are missing out. It's made with Moscato, peach schnapps, pineapple and orange juice, and Sprite. It's just perfect with the salad. No pun intended."

She smiled inquiringly.

"Thank you, but, technically, I'm working so I'll stick to

lemon water." She pulled a notebook and pen from her bag and set them on the table.

Tony backed away quietly after taking their order.

"So, what else can you tell me about Bramwell that you think people around the state may not know and would encourage them to visit?" Taylor asked.

"Oh, my goodness. Bramwell is perfect for visitors of all kinds. Whether they are history buffs or outdoorsy, there is something for everyone. We have a lot of festivals, and there's the antique shops."

"Sounds like a busy place," Taylor said.

Blanche tilted her head to the side. "No, not really. I'd say it's really a laid-back kind of town, so it's best for those seeking a peaceful escape. My favorite thing to do is a scenic drive during our fall, foliage season. Nothing busy or chaotic around here."

"You must have some good stories stored up," Taylor encouraged.

She beamed. "I sure do. I like to tell newcomers about the historic Bank of Bramwell. Way back when it was first started, the bank's janitor used to transport leather bags filled with money by wheelbarrow to the train depot. Right along the very brick-paved streets we still have."

"A lot of money in this town, huh?"

Blanche nodded emphatically. "Absolutely. For such a small county, it was thought to be quite thrilling that there were as many as nineteen millionaires residing here who made their fortunes from the local coalfields. Of course, at first not many outsiders knew of the town, but one of the stories tells of a telephone operator who would spend her days calling everyone she knew to tell them to come to Bramwell."

"I bet she was a pistol."

"Rumor has it she was. Supposedly part of her spiel was the humble brag that the local pharmacy carried Chanel No. 5. Used to be Bryant Pharmacy but now it's called something else. They were the third drugstore in America to carry the perfume."

"That's quite a surprise for such a small town so far from the big cities. Sounds like Bramwell was a winner from the beginning."

Blanche looked contemplative for a moment. "Bramwell has had its share of bad luck, too. A fire in 1910 wiped out most of the town, but they rebuilt. Then, of course, most of the wealthy families lost their fortunes in the stock market crash of 1929."

Taylor nodded. "Yes, I think that was the story of most small towns around America back then. So many rags to riches and right back to rags again."

Tony brought their soup and, as they sipped at it like ladies at tea, Taylor asked Blanche more about the history of her town, immediately mentally dismissing every word she said even as she took a few meaningless notes. She couldn't care less about their history but, when the salads came, it was time to pivot. As she choked down bites of things she'd never put in a salad—like shallots and candied pecans, and, dear God, goat cheese crumbles—she moved the conversation gently into what was everyone's favorite subject.

Themselves.

"That's all so interesting, but tell me about you, Blanche. How did you come to be giving tours of Bramwell's Millionaire Row?"

Blanche sat back in her seat and wiped her mouth.

"I'm part of the Bramwell Garden Club. That's just what we do, and I'm a team player. Well, we do a lot more than that, but I'm good at the tours so I probably do more than my share. I like talking to people. Keeps my mind off the hard parts of life."

"Have you had some hard parts?" Taylor asked sympathetically, then popped a strawberry into her mouth, but only after she'd separated it from a piece of arugula. She didn't know in what world someone thought lettuce and strawberries should be in the same mouthful, but it certainly wasn't hers.

Blanche shrugged. "Not more than most, I suppose. I've had a pretty good life and probably have more than I deserve, as my daddy used to say, including a nice roof over my head and three healthy sons."

"Three?" Taylor raised her eyebrows appreciatively, hiding her confusion. Kathie had said four sons. And she hadn't found any death certificates for any of them. "Lucky mama. But wasn't that a handful? You didn't mention a husband."

"Oh, I had one of those, too. He died about sixteen years ago. Massive heart attack took him in his sleep. Left me a widow with too much time on my hands. But my boys, they've been there for me every step of the way."

"I'd love to hear about them."

Yes, Blanche, keep talking.

Blanche sipped her sangria—her second round— and leaned in, her eyes sparkling with maternal pride. "They're all unique. As children tend to be."

"Tell me more," Taylor said, quite convincingly.

"First, there's James," Blanche began. "He's the oldest, a real go-getter. Graduated early from Georgetown University with a degree in business. He's married to a lovely woman named Natalie, and they have two adorable children, Lillian and Corey. James works as a financial analyst in Richmond."

"That sounds impressive," Taylor remarked.

Blanche chuckled. "Oh, it is. I wish they lived closer, but maybe one day. Then I have my second son, Daniel. He's the creative one. He studied film at NYU, you know, and now he's living in Los Angeles, working as a director. He's married to an actress named Sarah, and they're expecting their first child soon."

"Wow, a director in the family, that must be exciting," Taylor said. "And NYU? Blanche, you left out the little detail that your family must be one of the owners of a place on Millionaire Row."

She laughed. "Not quite, but we do alright." She lowered her head toward Taylor, and her voice. "There was a lot more money before sending three kids through college, that's for sure. But hopefully our sacrifices will mean I'll never find myself staring at a wall in a nursing home."

"Amen to that," Taylor said. "They owe you."

"Well, I don't like to think of it that way. I'm sure they'll do the right thing when I'm too old to care for myself. They're good boys. Especially my youngest, Samuel. He was his father's favorite, though Henry never let on to the other boys. Samuel is a bit of a free spirit. He pursued his passion for the environment and studied environmental science. He now works for an environmental nonprofit in Macon, Georgia."

Bingo. Taylor knew which one she needed to follow up on.

Free spirit. Located in Atlanta.

That was close enough. Samuel might be her first suspect.

Blanche continued. "Samuel has a life partner. He and Jeffery have been together for nearly five years now since he came out. It was a bit of a shock for his brothers, but I always knew it. A mother just knows these things. Do you understand what I mean?"

Taylor instantly felt deflated. It wasn't impossible that a gay man could be a rapist of women, but it was quite a long shot. She was going to have to dig deeper on all of them.

"Yes, I understand. Your sons all sound amazing," Taylor said, thinking they sounded a bit too good to be true. There had to be some skeletons she was hiding. A mother of sons didn't raise all angels. "You must be very proud of them."

Blanche beamed with pride. "I am, truly. They're all doing well, and I've got grandchildren to spoil. What more could a woman want?"

"It's quite a legacy you are building. Blanche, if you don't mind sharing, I'd love to hear how you and your husband met. It doesn't have to go in the article if you prefer."

Tony came back around with Blanche's third sangria, which

she greedily accepted then waved him away, as though —less than an hour before—she wasn't fawning about his attention. She took a long sip, then hesitated for a moment, her eyes glancing around as if checking for prying ears. Then, with a soft smile, she leaned closer to Taylor. "Well, darling, it's not something most people know, and I've never really shared it publicly. But I feel like I can trust you, so here it is."

"I'm listening," Taylor said, grinning. Today she was appreciative of alcohol. It was quite the truth serum at times.

Blanche leaned in and began to weave the tale of her teenage years. "You see, when I was just a young girl working the perfume counter at a drugstore in a big town about a hundred miles from here, I met a man who would change my life forever."

Taylor's curiosity deepened. "A man from Bramwell?"

Blanche nodded, her eyes distant as she recalled the memories. "Yes, his name was Henry. Eldest son of the Bramwell Wagners, and that's a big deal. They're old money," she whispered dramatically. "His father was a railroad tycoon. Anyway, Henry was a bit older than me, but that didn't matter. We met when he was in my town on a boys' golfing weekend and came into the drugstore looking to buy perfume to appease his sweetheart for being away."

Taylor raised an eyebrow, sensing a twist in the story. "And what happened next?"

Blanche chuckled, her cheeks tinged with a faint blush. "Well, I suppose you could say he had a change of heart. He and I struck up a conversation as I helped him pick out the perfect scent, and, before long, he was smitten with me. He took me out to dinner that very night. I can even remember what I wore. My cousin let me borrow her satin black cocktail dress that showed my shoulders, a daring move back then. We danced after dinner, too."

Taylor pretended to smile at the romantic turn of events. "So, he dumped his steady girlfriend for you?"

Blanche nodded, her eyes sparkling with a mix of nostalgia and embarrassment. "Yes, but it wasn't a girlfriend. It was his fiancée and it caused quite a stir here in town. He ignored the naysayers, and we had a whirlwind romance, then a magical wedding surrounded by our families and friends. Henry's family didn't approve of our union at first because they'd expected him to marry the perfect Miss Julia, from the Foxworth family, but love conquers all, as they say."

She held the remnants of her drink up and swirled the glass. She was looking tipsy.

"His father sent us away after we married. Once Henry earned his degree in finance, we came back and, eventually, he took over managing all the family banking and investments. He grew his father's money beyond what they ever dreamed of, and they never looked down on me again."

Taylor had to wonder about that, considering the bitter expression Blanche wore.

"And what ever happened to Julia?"

Blanche looked even more sullen. "Old Julia Powell turned into a spinster, as they said in the old days. Some say she never got over my Henry and pined after him until he was dead. She stayed here in Bramwell and never moved away, just to spite me. I had to dance around her for my whole adult life."

"She's gone, too?"

"Don't I wish," Blanche said. "But I got the last laugh. Talk about nursing homes—she's doing hard time in the Bramwell Meadows right now, probably rocking on the porch, wearing a wet diaper. While I'm sitting here at this nice restaurant enjoying my Sangria and wearing my favorite Tom Ford silk shirt."

Oh, yes. Blanche was tipsy. Maybe even drunk.

Taylor could see the ugly coming out in her, and it wasn't just from the alcohol. She thought about the man who had invaded her privacy. Her body.

It made sense that Blanche's evil streak was passed down to one of her sons.

And now she had one more stop to make before they left town.

CHAPTER 18

*T*he Bramwell nursing home was a stately but somewhat faded building nestled in the bend of a line of trees on the outskirts of town. Contrary to what Blanche had said, there wasn't a porch or any rocking chairs, either. Just a grand covered entrance with meticulous landscaping.

They parked the truck, and Taylor left Sam and Alice there, promising them she'd be quick, then entered the building.

Alice looked happy enough. Sam had taken her for hotdogs and shakes, then they did some shopping downtown. He'd bought her a sweatshirt and some beaded bracelets, and they were both smiling when Taylor showed up in an Uber. She'd talked Blanche into doing the same, even ordering and paying for hers, too, to keep her from getting behind the wheel in the tipsy shape she was in.

Inside, the receptionist greeted her warmly. Taylor approached the desk with a sense of purpose. "Hi, I'm Taylor Gray and I'm here to visit Mrs. Julia Powell. Is she available?"

The receptionist checked her records and nodded. "Yes, she is here but it's Ms. Powell. If I can just get some information from you first."

She took Taylor's driver's license and made a copy, then jotted down her phone number before handing her a visitor's pass.

"You can find her in Room 203 on the second floor."

Taylor took a deep breath and made her way up to the second floor. She found Room 203 and knocked gently before entering.

Inside, she expected to find a frail, senile old lady, but she was in for a surprise. Julia, though elderly, had a sharp look in her eyes and a presence that defied her years. She was fully dressed, with even a dab of lipstick on and her hair in a neat bun. She sat at a small table in the corner of her room, putting together a puzzle that looked to have a million or more pieces. Or at least too many for Taylor to even think about trying. Puzzles were her downfall.

"Ms. Powell?" Taylor asked tentatively.

Julia turned her gaze toward Taylor, her expression curious but guarded. "Who are you, dear?"

"I'm Taylor Gray," she replied, "and I'm doing a journalistic piece about Bramwell. I heard you might have some interesting stories about influential people in town."

Julia's demeanor softened, and she motioned for Taylor to take a seat. "Well, I suppose I do know a few things. Who would you like to hear about?"

Taylor thought for a moment. "Could you tell me about some of the influential families in Bramwell?"

Julia nodded, her eyes distant as she reminisced. "Certainly. There's the Worthington family, who have been pillars of this community for generations. They own the largest coal mining operation in the region. And then there's the Caldwell family, prominent in politics and law. They've produced a senator."

Taylor took notes as Julia spoke, realizing that she was getting valuable insights into the town's history. "And what about the Wagners?"

At the mention of the Wagners, Julia's demeanor shifted. She became quiet, her gaze fixed on a distant point. Taylor could sense that this was a sensitive topic.

Julia finally spoke, her voice tinged with sadness. "Ah, the Wagners. Henry Wagner was a good man. I miss him dearly. He was my best friend, you know."

The way she said it made Taylor think that perhaps Henry hadn't completely dumped Julia after all. She was staring at the window, seemingly lost in thought.

"How did you come to know Henry?" Tayler asked, pretending ignorance.

Julia looked her straight in the eye. "I knew him way before Blanche came into the picture. We were deeply in love once upon a time. Before she ruined it by using her youth and deceptive ways to steal him from me."

Her words were bitter, but her tone was even and matter of fact, as though she'd come to terms with it.

"I'm sorry to hear that. Could you tell me more about her and Henry?"

Julia sighed, her eyes welling up with old emotions. "Once she got her claws into him, he married her and that meant our romance was over, but she couldn't break our bond. Henry and I remained close friends and confidantes until right before his death. He was going to leave her finally. The kids were grown, and he'd decided he'd given her enough of himself."

Taylor didn't know what to say. She wasn't expecting to get such private details, though she was glad she'd come. Now she had to try to work her way around to what Julia could tell her about the sons.

"I'm sorry," she said.

Julia nodded. "Me too. He told her he was leaving, and she knew why. He thought he'd kept our friendship a secret all these years, but she knew. She threatened that, if he left, she'd ruin his reputation and his relationship with his sons. His sons were everything to him and she is nasty enough to follow through, so he backed out of leaving her."

"Then he died of a heart attack."

Julia's eyes went from sad to fiery. "No. He died of a broken heart. And now I am, too. Dying ... slowly. Much slower than he did, but we'll be together soon. In the meantime, I hope that Blanche is happy with herself. She sent him to his early death. And, believe me, she wasn't always the buttoned-up and proper lady she portrays herself to be. She's got a little problem with the sauce. Henry has had to deal with it for decades. She's even been in treatment. Some fancy rehab in Florida. Came back with a good tan but didn't help her affliction none."

"Oh, that's unfortunate," Taylor said.

Julia leaned in. "Sure is, but that's not their biggest secret. I guess with Henry on the wrong side of the dirt, I can tell someone now. You see, she was pregnant when he met her, but he didn't know it. I heard it from a friend who heard it from her cousin who heard it from her mama. When I told him, he almost called off the engagement, but, to keep him, she gave that baby away."

Bingo. Taylor felt a tingle go through her fingers and up her arms.

Her eyes widened in feigned shock. "Wait, there's another child, a fourth child?"

Of course, there's a fourth. Kathie Huff said so.

Julia nodded solemnly. "Yes, it was a boy. Not his, and this was a secret between Blanche and Henry, but there were never secrets between he and I. She wanted to present herself as the perfect wife and mother, so they kept it hidden from the world. Henry wouldn't let her do anything drastic to the child, because, like I said, he was a good man. He would've raised it as his own, but his parents would've never forgiven him, or accepted the child. Blanche agreed that they needed a fresh start. She went away until it was born and then gave it up for adoption."

"Why would he go through with the marriage once he knew that?" Taylor asked. Her mind was spinning, already laying next steps to try to find out if there were adoption records.

"Because his parents were already against him marrying her and, once I told him about her being with child, he was too proud to let them know they were right. He and his father always had a sort of battle going on. It was his pride, Taylor. He gave up on our love because of his reckless pride." She looked down at Taylor's hand, noting the ring on her finger. "You'll find out for yourself one day. A man will let his pride wreck his life, if his woman can't be strong enough to stand up to him and make him see what's right. I wish I'd have been stronger. I would've lived a much different life. Now, if you don't mind, that's enough reminiscing for me today. I'd like to get back to my puzzle, where every piece has a promised place and fate has nothing to do with where it lands."

"Of course. I really appreciate you chatting with me, Ms. Powell. I just have one more question, if you would humor me."

"What is that, dear?" She yawned, then excused her bad manners.

"Do you have any idea where that baby ended up?"

CHAPTER 19

*T*aylor stared at the two brothers sitting across from her and the lawyer who was representing them both. Shane had wanted to question them separately, but she'd talked him into following her plan. If she was right, it would work out. If she was wrong, they were back to square one. They didn't have the results of the partial handprint back yet, but something told her it wasn't going to be conclusive anyway. There wasn't enough of it to analyze, in her opinion, so they couldn't depend on it as solid evidence.

Over the last few days, she'd interviewed six more teenagers. Friends of both Marc and Larson, as well as a few of Larson's past girlfriends. She talked to the school counselor and more teachers of both the boys. Everyone in the faculty that she talked to said about the same thing: Marc was trouble and Larson was an easy kid. She talked to the aunt again, who solidified some of Taylor's ideas about the brothers. Overall, the feedback was interesting, though less than ground-breaking. Still, every detail she gathered about the boys was beginning to give her a gut feeling.

One thing was for certain. They were very bonded. Not only Larson and Marc to each other, but to their little sister, too.

It was a tough case, and the community was starting to get antsy for an arrest. The sheriff had given them only the rest of the week, then he was calling in other agencies. If he did that, she'd be delegated to a paper pusher on the case.

They had to break it and break it now.

"Before we start, I have to advise you of your Miranda rights," Shane said. He quickly went through them. He had the crime scene photos and he brought them out and slapped them on the table in front of the boys. "Look at this," he ordered.

Larson winced and looked away. Marc stared at the photos angrily. He had not come to the interview willingly and was going to make sure everyone knew it.

"After years of being good parents and responsible pillars of the community, this is their legacy," he said, tapping a photo aggressively. "From now on, when people think of your parents, they won't remember the good things they've done, or their commitment to living life right, they'll only think of the gruesome way they died."

"That's a bit harsh, don't you think, Detective Weaver?" the lawyer said.

"Harsh, but true," Shane said, his gaze steely.

He could be stone cold when he wanted to, but this was it. They needed to get at the emotions to force their hand. Clayton Davis wasn't their man. He was a womanizer and a thief, but not a killer. She had no doubt that the murders were personal. It was time to push the boys.

"We have the phone records," Shane said.

Marc shrugged. Larson's look was impassive.

They'd finally gotten the phone records, but the only thing it showed was that Marc had called Larson that night around eleven. He also had some calls and texting back and forth to his girlfriend. After that, nothing. The phone didn't travel, either. But that meant nothing. With so many true crime shows now, everyone knew, if you planned to commit a crime, don't take your phone or it will pinpoint everywhere you've been.

"Marc, you called Larson at 11:17 p.m.," Shane said.

He stared back at Shane.

"Is that a question for my client?" the lawyer said.

"Why didn't you text?" Taylor said. "Usually, you text back and forth. On that night, you chose to call instead."

"Wanted to hear his voice. Is that a crime?" Marc said. "You try being locked away from your family for months and see if you don't want to talk to them once in a while."

"Not a crime, but suspicious," Shane said.

"Patty and Willis at the facility were very forthcoming, after some persuasion," Taylor said. "Turns out, any patient with a bit of money to spare can arrange to leave the grounds for a few hours or even most of the night, as long as they're back before morning bed count."

The lawyer was doing his best to look bored, but Taylor could see they'd hit a nerve with him. "You have no evidence that my client, Marc Swanson, ever left that facility on the night in question. If you did, you'd show it now," he said.

"Think what you want," Shane said. "We don't have to show anything yet. We're just talking, aren't we?"

"Here's what I think, Marc," Taylor said. "First, I'm sorry about your childhood. It sucked. There's no getting around that. When you were adopted by the Swansons, you thought you'd finally gotten past all the traumas. But it was so deep, you couldn't let it go."

"What is this crap?" Larson said. "Psychoanalyzing my brother?"

"Just let her talk," the lawyer said.

Taylor continued, her gaze on Marc. "Your aunt said you've

been a challenge from the get-go. That you butted heads with your parents all the time. They wanted you to be a devout Catholic like them, but you weren't used to such rigid disciplinarians."

"My dad bullied him," Larson said protectively.

"It that what he did, Marc?" Shane asked, leaning in. "Bullied you until you just couldn't take it anymore? It had to be the last straw when they filed to have you made a ward of the state again. But they'd only met a wall when they asked the state to place you with another family. They say they loved you but couldn't handle you, but you didn't want to do it all again. Be rejected once more by yet more people who claimed to want to be your family. Did you, Marc?"

He was getting to him. Marc's face was turning the colors of rage. Larson was shifting in his seat uncomfortably. He looked like he wanted to say something.

"When you started high school, things got worse," Taylor kept on to Marc. "Your aunt said that you have a deviant personality. That you can't form emotional bonds like Larson and Abby can. You were eight years old when they found you and had already been through six foster homes. You were damaged beyond redemption."

"Not true," Larson said. "He and I have an unbreakable bond. Marc would do anything for me. And Abby, too."

Yep, that's what Taylor was counting on.

"After that, you rebelled worse. Didn't you, Marc?" Shane asked. "All the way until they had you placed into the mental health facility. A much-deserved break for them but pure hell for you to be separated from your siblings. Your girlfriend. All your friends."

"The school counselor labeled you *profoundly troubled*," Taylor added. "You told a friend that you could walk up to your dad and put a knife in his back easily. Especially for all the creative punishments he heaped on you for every tiny offense. Hell, I can see why you'd want to do it, too. I heard all about the stump incident."

"A bit coincidental that the same maul you were using during that evening of cruel punishment is the same one used to deal the final blow to send your mother to her death, isn't it?" Taylor said.

She let that sink in for a moment.

"This is what we believe happened. You convinced Patty and Willis to let you have a few free hours. You called Larson to let him know to leave the door unlocked and to stay in his room," she said.

Marc started shaking his head.

She continued. "You got there, and your mom was in her usual place for that time of night, the recliner downstairs, in front of the television. You snuck up behind her, reached around and stabbed her in the throat. That's where the huge puddle of blood downstairs came from."

Larson put his hands over his eyes, lowering his head.

"Please, stop," he said, his voice agonized.

Marc was silently defiant. The lawyer sat with his arms crossed over his chest, his expression livid.

Taylor leaned forward. "But it didn't kill her. She couldn't scream but she still had some fight left in her and she struggled. You stabbed her again and she dropped to the floor. Your dad heard the commotion and came running. He tried to fight you off through the house, hence the defensive wounds on his hands. You stabbed him repeatedly, finally getting him in the heart. When he was down, you went back to your mother, and she was gone."

"This is where it gets really ugly," Shane said. "You looked outside and saw Kimberly running through the yard, probably going for help. You chased her through the woods, running her down. We found the blood trail. Then you walked her back home, where you finished her off with the maul. The very one that your father used to punish you last winter. Your final symbol of rebellion against him."

"You're sick," Marc said, nearly spitting the words through his teeth.

"No, what's sick is that killing her wasn't enough," Shane said. "Then you had to undress her, assault her, and leave her naked but for one sock, in a humiliating pose to be found by strangers."

Larson was rocking back and forth now, crying. Marc reached over and put his arm around him.

"Don't listen to them. It's not true," he murmured.

"But one mistake you made," Taylor said. "Well, two actually. First, you didn't count on so much screaming. Little Abby woke up and looked out the window to see you carrying the axe. And two, on your way out the door to chase your mother, you left your bloody handprint on the glass. Did you know that handprints are like fingerprints? No two are alike."

She left out the fact that they didn't have the analysis back.

"Larson had a new set of clothes ready for you downstairs. You washed off outside and changed, then dumped the bloody clothes on the way back to the facility. You were in and out in just under three hours, back in bed before morning head count," Shane said.

"What is all this grandstanding?" The lawyer asked. "You've concocted a fantasy timeline to fit your own needs, without a shred of evidence. Now, if you don't have any questions for my clients, then it's time we go."

Larson looked up, his expression now one of hope.

"You can go, but Marc will be staying with us," Shane said. "Hopefully he'll find our accommodations as comfortable as those at the facility."

That got all their attention.

"For what?" Marc and Larson said at the same time.

"On what grounds?" The lawyer asked.

Now Taylor was really nervous. If Shane followed through

with her plan and it didn't work, Shane would be left looking like an idiot. It could even end his career.

But if he didn't ...

"Two counts of capital murder," Shane said, then went through with the last act. He pulled his handcuffs from his belt and plopped them on the table, the metal against the wood echoing in the room like a gunshot.

"Wait," Marc said. "I didn't do it."

"Tell it to the judge," Shane said, then stood and came around the table. "Stand up and put your hands behind your back."

Marc jumped to his feet, finally showing some fear. He put his arms behind him, and Shane clicked the handcuffs on.

Larson pushed back from the table and shrieked. An anguished bellow that came from the depths of his soul as he bent over his lap, crying.

"Let him go," he cried. "It wasn't Marc. It was me. I did it. I killed them."

The room went silent other than the wracking sobs coming from Larson.

Finally, the lawyer found his head and stood in front of Larson's chair. "Don't say another word. Not one damn word."

Larson looked up at him, his face tear streaked. "It's over. I can't do this anymore. All I wanted was a family to want me forever, and they were going to do the same thing to me. They only cared about Abby. Marc and I were a burden. I wanted them to love me. Just *love* me."

"Oh my God, Larson. No. Please ... no, no," Marc said, his voice pleading. "You couldn't have. You don't have that in you."

Shane took the handcuffs off Marc, and he grabbed his brother, pulling him from his chair and into his arms. They stood there crying together.

Larson wept like no one Taylor had ever heard weep.

Taylor felt a burden of sorrow for the broken boy. Yes, he was a murderer, but she had no doubt it was extenuating circumstances. That didn't absolve him from what he did, and he at least had the morals enough not to send his brother to prison for his crime.

"You've confessed now, Larson. You'll feel better if you just tell it all. Get it out of your system," Shane said.

"My client does not want to talk anymore," the lawyer said.

Larson pulled back from Marc. He spoke through ragged sobs. "Yes, I do. I'll say it all now and never speak of it again."

"Are you sure?" Marc asked him, looking into his eyes.

Larson nodded and rubbed at his face with his sleeve.

"If you do this, Larson, there's no taking it back," the lawyer said. "I advise against it."

"There's no taking back anything I've done," Larson said. "If there was, I'd have already done it."

"I'll pour you some water and we can finish this," Taylor said, pulling the pitcher and a glass close to her. Everyone was quiet while she poured one, then another, passing them to both boys.

Once Larson had taken a long drink, and calmed himself a bit, he looked ready. "It happened just like you said. Everything."

"How did the night start? Before the incident?" Shane asked.

"I brought home a bad grade. More than bad; I was failing Spanish," said Larson. "Mom told me that I couldn't use the car until I got the grade back up to passing. I was angry and I started drinking in my room. I was thinking about how she discarded Marc so easily, letting my dad just abandon him, and I realized that they were eventually going to do the same thing to me. Then Abby would be here all alone and wouldn't have us to protect her. I figured if something happened to my parents, they would place us somewhere else together and I could look out for her."

Taylor doubted that was the whole truth. Yes, he probably was very protective of Abby because it was obvious both boys were, but, in her gut, it was more likely that his teenage testosterone and hormones were out of control and his anger escalated until he could think of nothing else but revenge. Very tragic ... and could have been so avoidable.

She wished more families would get counseling before things escalated to this level. Now three children were orphans again, and two good people dead. Larson would spend the rest of his life in prison. Abby would go back to foster care, and she wasn't sure what would happen to Marc.

She only knew that their happily ever after was done. She thought back to their first questioning of Larson, when he was at the neighbor's house with his sister. He was so calm. So methodical. She hoped it was only shock, and that he wasn't as cold-blooded as that made him look now.

"But why Mom, Larson?" Marc whispered, shaking his head. He didn't sound angry, just confused. And so very sad. "And did you have to—"

"—don't say it. I know, man. I'm sorry. I was drunk and I just lost it. You don't know what it was like without you there. Dad—he just took it all out on me." His head was lowered but he looked up quickly, locking gazes with Marc. "But I did not assault her. Not like that. Like everyone thinks. I just thought, if I stripped her, then it would look more like a stranger did it. I'm so sorry."

Marc looked sick to his stomach. It was clear to Taylor that he wasn't involved, though she'd already come to that conclusion. She'd had to do a lot of talking to convince Shane, and had to lay it all out several times. There were some very strong indicators that Larson was lying from the beginning.

Starting with the 911 call when he'd said he thought his parents were dead.

He'd only seen his mother out the window, according to his story, and had not ventured through the rest of the house. But Mr. Swanson was dead in the study.

Luckily, Shane had decided to give her theory and her strategy a chance, and it had worked.

"The palm print?" Marc asked.

Larson nodded slowly. "Yes, it's mine. I didn't know I left it, or I would've cleaned it up before I went upstairs."

"Where are the clothes and the other murder weapon?" Shane asked.

"I can show you. Just down the block down a path in the woods."

CHAPTER 20

*T*aylor poured the sugar into the pitcher, then covered it with the saucepan of brewed tea. Carefully she mixed it up, added water to the top of the rim, then put the lid on and set it in the refrigerator to cool.

When she turned around, Cate was sitting at the table. She was so quiet that Taylor hadn't heard her. Without a word, she got two glasses out and put ice in them, then poured sweet tea and sat down at the table, placing one glass in front of Cate.

She accepted the glass with a weak smile and took a sip. Taylor noticed she had a new, wide streak of gray hair that ran from her temple down to her shoulder.

The silence hung between them for a moment until Cate broke it.

"How's Sam?" she asked.

"He's good. I'm surprised you didn't see him. He's outside with Alice, teaching her how to exercise the dogs safely. She wants to earn money for her own phone, so he's making her work for it."

Cate nodded approvingly. "That's good. It's important for kids to learn the value of hard work. Seems these days they all have all the latest technology—computers, phones. And it's just an automatic thing. They don't have to work for it."

"Yeah," Taylor agreed. "She's a good kid, though. I bet he buys her one anyway before she leaves. She's using his old one, but she can't do much on it."

"Do you know when she's going back?"

Taylor shook her head. "No, but at least not until one of her parents comes home. Wesley up at Family Services worked it out with her county. They've opened an investigation over there, and the other two kids are with a grandmother. When Alice's mom gets out of the hospital, she's going to have to answer for taking off like she did."

"Good," Cate said. "She should. Too much can happen these days and you can't just run off and leave three kids home alone. I don't care if she is twelve. As she proved, there are some things she doesn't have the maturity level to handle."

"But, Mom, how are things with you and Ellis?"

Cate's expression grew somber. "We've had a few short phone calls, but that's about it. He's been busy with his new home build."

Taylor could sense that there was more to it than just a busy schedule. "Mom, you can tell me. Is everything okay between you two?"

Cate hesitated, her eyes welling up with tears. "Not really. Honestly, Taylor, I thought coming out of prison, I'd focus on being with my daughters and grandkids. I never thought I'd take a chance on love again. I shouldn't have let my guard down."

Taylor reached across the table and placed her hand over Cate's. "Mom, you have us. You have me and my sisters. You're not alone."

Cate managed a weak smile. "I know. And I promise, that's more than enough. Because romantic love ... it's a complicated thing. I've seen so many women in prison, like this one lady I knew who did time for a crime her husband committed. She pined after him for years, and he mollified her with promises.

But when she got out, she found out he'd moved on. New woman, kids, the whole thing. After she'd given him twenty-some years of her life and devotion."

Taylor's heart ached for her mother. "I'm so sorry, Cate. But not all of them are bad. Look at Sam. He's a good guy."

Cate took Taylor's hand and held it tightly. "I hope so, honey. But promise me one thing. Save a tiny part of yourself, just in case. Don't give it all away and, if you are ever left alone again, you'll have something to start over with."

Tears welled up in Taylor's eyes as she gazed at her mother, now so broken by her past experiences. She nodded silently, understanding the cautionary tale Cate had shared. She also knew from experience that love was indeed a complex and risky venture, but she hoped her relationship with Sam would be different.

"I'll be careful," she promised.

"I heard you and Shane cracked the Swanson case," Cate said, changing the subject. "Such a tragedy about the boy."

"Yeah, it's sad, but I'm glad he did the right thing. Everyone thought it was Marc and, if Larson hadn't confessed, who knows if his brother would've taken the heat for it."

"What did Shane think? Were you both on the same page?"

Taylor smiled softly. "Well, let's just say it took a lot of convincing for him to allow us to try getting a confession my way. He didn't think that Larson had it in him to do something so heinous, but, turns out, from the outside looking in, he was the star child, but there was more going on than everyone realized."

"There always is," Cate said. "Some of the families that people envy the most are the ones hiding the biggest secrets."

Her statement made Taylor think of Anna, and all she'd been hiding behind the façade of her upscale lifestyle. In the time she'd been divorced, she'd slowly let more stories out, a little at a time and, turns out, she'd been very unhappy. She'd held it together so long for the kids, who she thought she'd been fooling, but who were just as unhappy as she was living a lie. They were all so much happier now.

"The handprint came back yesterday," Taylor said. "It was Larson's. But even with that, he could've created a new narrative in which he tried to help his mother and put his hand on the glass door. We needed that confession."

Cate looked really interested.

"Can I ask you a question, Taylor?"

"Sure."

"At what point did you suspect Larson when everyone else had his brother pegged as their prime suspect?"

"Really from the beginning I had suspicions about him that kept niggling the back of my mind," Taylor said. "In his initial story, he said he came straight downstairs, looked out the window and saw his mother, and called. I went back to the crime scene several times, with and without Shane. I found it was impossible to see the place where Kimberly's body lay from the window without getting on the counter and looking directly below. I moved to the dining room, and you couldn't see anywhere near that spot. Then I thought, well ... he's a kid. It was a traumatizing moment and maybe he forgot something or was confused, so I gave him the benefit of the doubt. But the 911 call in which he was so calm and said he thought both parents were dead was a big deal that I couldn't get past."

Cate nodded. "That makes sense. He's a kid. You can't forecast how they'll react in an emergency."

"Right. But the more people close to him that I interviewed, the more things just started stacking up. Some of his friends told me that, lately, Larson has been getting in more trouble with his dad and that it upset him pretty bad. The aunt said that when Larson was adopted by Bishop and Kimberly, for years they'd find him awake in the middle of the night, wandering around just to check and make sure everyone was still there, that he hadn't been abandoned again."

"Oh, wow. That's sad. How old was he when he was adopted?"

"Seven. But he'd been in the system since he was four. She said he had a lot of emotional problems and had been abused in some of his previous foster homes. Said it was disturbing how hard he worked to be the perfect child, trying to stay in his parent's good graces, then, when things started falling apart and Marc was sent away, he began to regress and have nightmares. He dreamed about his life with his prostitute mother. About being hungry. Alone. He got so paranoid that Kimberly and Bishop didn't love him anymore, he snapped."

"Heartbreaking. I hope they'll get him some help," Cate said. "And that poor little girl. What will happen to her?"

"If a family member doesn't take her, unfortunately it'll be back to the system until they find her another home. She's going to need a lot of therapy, too. The whole thing is tragic. I'll be glad to close the books on this one so I can try to get it out of my head." Taylor dropped her head in her hands and rubbed at her eyes.

"I'm really proud of you, Taylor," Cate said softly.

Taylor looked up. For so many years, she'd dreamed of having a parent say those words. She never imagined it would be the mother who she'd thought had died in a fire. The Swanson's story was dramatic and tragic, just like the Gray's had once been. But at least her own story was turning around and gaining ground as a potential to be a happily ever after.

She hadn't lost hope yet.

"Thank you. That means a lot to hear you say that," she finally said. "Dad has never approved of my choice of career."

"Well, he always could be a stubborn ass at times," Cate said, chuckling. "I do have to take up for him a bit though. With what they did to us in our own investigation, then sending me to prison for something I didn't do, and leaving him to raise four girls alone, he doesn't trust anyone official."

"That was a whole different agency for a fire investigation, but, yeah, I get it. Some see us as one and the same."

The door flew open, and Sam came in, startling them both.

"Taylor, can you come out here? I just checked my phone, and Lois called fifteen minutes ago and said Derek is on his way over and will be here any minute."

A chorus of barking told them their guest had arrived. And they all stepped outside. Cecil came out of the boarding kennels, too, to see what was going on. As they stepped onto the gravel driveway, their eyes fell upon Derek, Alice's father. He was a tall, imposing figure with an air of detachment that seemed to envelop him like a shroud. His strong, angular face bore the wear and tear of a life filled with hardship, and his dark hair was impeccably combed. He wore a somber, black suit that hung heavily on his frame, a strange choice of clothing considering what Taylor knew his job to be.

Alice had seen her father's car approaching and had walked toward him to meet at the gate, Diesel at her side. When she reached him, the interaction looked anything but warm. Derek's cold, distant gaze locked onto Alice, his lips forming a thin line that betrayed no hint of affection. He extended a hand over the gate to rest it on her shoulder, but the touch looked more obligatory than comforting. Their conversation was terse and marked by an unmistakable tension.

Sam, Taylor, and Cate watched from a distance, the atmosphere heavy with unspoken dread. Cate's suggestion to give them a minute seemed appropriate, for it was clear that Derek was there for something important.

Suddenly, Alice turned to look at them.

Sam took one step toward her, and she took off running. Taylor thought she was running to him, but Alice kept going, straight on by all of them. When she passed, they could see a river of tears running down her face, but she kept going, pumping her arms as fast as she could.

Diesel ran beside her, not letting her get even one step ahead, though Alice's gaze was fixed on the tree line, like she didn't realize he was there.

"What was that?" Sam said, turning to look at Taylor with a confused expression.

"I don't know. You'd better go after Alice. I'll go talk to Derek and see what he told her."

⁂

SAM JOGGED QUICKLY AFTER ALICE, but she beat him to the lake and had launched a kayak into the water and was paddling out furiously. Diesel was barking up a storm, which was unusual. He was used to them taking the kayaks out and he usually happily played in the shallows if he wasn't allowed to go. But not this time.

He was making his displeasure known.

"Hold on, boy," Sam called. "I'm coming."

Diesel looked back but then took a leap into the deeper water and began swimming in Alice's direction.

As Sam jumped into another kayak, paddling furiously after Alice, he was sick with worry. Diesel's frantic barks echoed across the water as he tried to reach her, too.

He called out to Alice, his voice laced with concern. "Alice! Slow down! Let me catch up!"

Alice, however, seemed driven by an unyielding need to escape. She had already covered a considerable distance, her kayak cutting through the water like a desperate plea for solace. Sam pushed himself harder, determined to reach her, his paddles slicing through the water with each powerful stroke. For such a small person, she was making easy work of the kayaking.

"Stop, Alice. Diesel is getting tired. Let him catch up," he yelled.

That did it. She wouldn't risk letting anything happen to an animal because of her.

As he closed the gap, he could see the tears streaming down Alice's face, her body trembling with the effort she was exerting. Diesel, now swimming beside her, seemed equally distressed. She reached down and pet him, and he licked her hand, even as he kept moving.

Alice suddenly lay over the front of the kayak, her sobs wracking her body. Sam drew nearer, his concern deepening as he watched her heart-wrenching display of grief.

"Alice," he called gently. "It's going to be okay. We'll figure this out, no matter what your dad said. Talk to me. What happened?"

Alice turned to him, her eyes red and swollen from crying. She struggled to speak through her tears. "My mom ... she's dead," she choked out, her voice filled with devastation. "She killed herself an hour after they released her from psychiatric care."

Sam's anger flared at Derek's callousness in delivering such devastating news without professional support or guidance. He wanted to go back and throttle him, but Alice needed comfort and reassurance in that moment.

He pulled up close, then reached down and pulled Diesel onto his kayak.

Diesel splayed out, then threw up lake water and collapsed.

"Stay put, boy," Sam said. Then he gently reached over and touched Alice's shoulder.

"I'm so sorry, Alice," he said softly. "I don't even know what to say. That's terrible news." He stumbled for words and wished for Taylor. She always knew what to say.

When he looked back, he saw her on the bank, her presence offering silent support. She wasn't close enough to hear, but Sam could feel her sending him strength.

He wasn't a father, but he reminded himself that he had a good one and had been through losing his mother, too. His dad hadn't tried to make it all go away, but he'd walked through the fire of emotions with him, never letting him feel alone.

That was something he could do with Alice.

He turned back around. "Alice, I can't promise you what the future holds, but this is what I can do. We'll find out for sure if I'm your dad, like you think I am. And, if I am, we'll figure out what's next. But one thing is certain—I'll be with you every step of the way as you get through this. Your mom would've wanted me to do that."

Alice nodded, but she didn't reply. He could see that she was crushed.

Even if she had a difficult family life, a kid always needed a mother.

"I talked to your mom a few weeks ago, Alice. Did you know that?" When she didn't answer, he continued. "She told me how proud she was of you and how much you've helped her over the years. With your brother and sister, and with just everything. She really loves you. She said you were like her little best friend. So, even if she didn't say it much, just remember that."

Alice looked up at him, and the depth of sorrow in her eyes cut him to the core. He hoped she wasn't going to call him a liar. Because that's exactly what he was.

"She told me that. Sometimes," she said, her voice barely above a whisper, "when she wasn't mad at Derek, she was a good mom."

"I'll bet she was," Sam said, glad Alice was talking again. He didn't think that Brooke had any good-mom-bones in her whole body, but he'd never tell Alice what he thought.

"I wish I could've told her that," Alice said, then crumbled into tears again. "I was angry at her for leaving again. I never said goodbye. Jane Eyre taught me to speak up for myself and that's why I'm not going back. But she also taught me to forgive. That love is more important than anything else and to forgive the important people in your life. I wish I could've seen my mom after I read the book."

He got his kayak as close as possible, then gathered her into his arms so she had somewhere to lay her head while she cried.

"I know, honey. I'm so sorry. She was a good one," he said. He didn't mind lying to Alice this once. She needed a new recollection of her mother. One that she could take into the future and hang on to when she missed her the most. One that would help her forget the bad times. Sam would help her form that memory.

That was the least he could do before Alice was ripped from his life and thrust back into her own. With her head on his shoulder and the rush of emotions transferring from her to him, hitting him deep in his soul, he realized now that, when that happened, it might just be the worst day of his life.

CHAPTER 21

*T*aylor arrived at Faire's house and there were so many cars in the driveway and parked in the street that she had to walk a good ten minutes from where she finally found a spot. As she approached, she saw Boone standing outside, looking unsure of himself. Boone was the town's well-known rambler, known for his intellectual disability. While some found his social behavior unsettling, most locals sympathized and looked out for him. In his mid-thirties, he had the cognitive abilities of a young child, stemming from a traumatic incident when he was eleven. He had accidentally shot off his thumb, which was replaced with his big toe due to medical delays and his father's reluctance to seek specialized care. Some say he didn't cry during the ordeal, though that might be an exaggeration.

"Hi, Boone," she greeted him. "How are you?"

He shuffled over to her and nodded rapidly. That meant he was doing okay.

Today he had his usual red and black flannel shirt tied around his waist. His suspenders held up his baggy jeans, but it appeared that he'd just had a haircut. The only one he'd let touch his head was Bessie, who worked downtown at the Hair Place. Taylor hoped she never retired, or Boone would never get a haircut again.

"Do you want to go in and see the art show?" she asked.

He shook his head.

Boone liked to be involved, but only if he didn't have to be close to too many people. Taylor knew from experience he also liked to be helpful. He'd found something of Joni Stott's that had been very important in the investigation of her death.

"Well, how about you do me a favor and watch the door? Make sure no one comes in who looks scary?"

Boone nodded and a small smile creeped up on his face before he quickly hid it.

"I can do that," he said.

"Thank you. When you come by the department, tell Dottie I said you get extra candy."

He beamed at that. He liked to stop by and pull from the lollipop bucket they kept for kids at the front desk.

"See you in a bit."

The minute she opened the door, she felt a sense of pride swelling in her chest. Lucy had done it. Everything looked spectacular.

A tasteful sign was on a stand in the grand foyer.

Soulful Strokes: Faire Tinsley's Mystical Masterpieces, it read.

She couldn't help but be amazed at how Lucy had pulled it all off. The foyer and the big, open room beyond—that was once Faire's living room—was adorned with ethereal decorations that complemented the mystical theme of the paintings. Soft, warm lighting bathed the room, casting a dreamy ambiance. Delicate fairy lights hung from the ceiling, creating a celestial glow that danced over the artwork.

A few seating areas had been set up, vintage chairs covered in red velvet, facing each other in the corners. A high-school-aged girl dressed in white shirt and black slacks walked around quietly, carrying a tray of smoked salmon pieces on tiny, toasted pieces of bread. Another held a tray of champagne.

She caught Taylor's attention with a nod.

"No, thank you," Taylor mouthed, and the girl moved on.

Clusters of guests milled about, sipping on glasses of red and white wine, and nibbling on the assortment of delectable treats displayed on an antique sideboard cabinet against the wall. Taylor recognized some of Hart's Ridge upper crust but was also glad to see some regular people, from families like hers, and was happy that they realized the gift of appreciating art is for everyone and has nothing to do with your tax bracket. The chatter in the room was a mixture of awe and admiration for the captivating artwork that adorned the walls.

As Taylor scanned the room, her eyes landed on Lucy, who looked elegant in a fitted black dress, her blonde hair pulled back in a sleek, low ponytail. This Lucy was a far cry from the pixie-like figure with a hammer that Taylor had seen the last time she'd visited the home.

Taylor was struck speechless.

Lucy caught her eye and made her way over, a confident smile playing on her artfully lined lips. Johnny wasn't anywhere in sight, which resurfaced the memory in Taylor's mind that Lucy had told her she was going to let Levi and the other kids babysit him for this event.

"Taylor, you made it!" Lucy said, her voice low and quiet, different than her usual tough inflection. "Isn't this amazing? I'm so proud of Faire."

Taylor nodded. "You've outdone yourself, Lucy. Everything looks incredible."

Lucy beamed. "Thanks, Taylor. It's been a lot of hard work, but it's all worth it to see her talent recognized like this."

"Who else is here? Jo and Anna? Cate? *Shane?*" She didn't mean to, but the last name ended with a sarcastic tone.

"As you already know, he couldn't come because he's working

on the Swanson case. But what is your deal with him and I, Taylor?" Lucy asked, her smile now gone and fire in her eyes. "We have to figure this out because I like him. Don't ruin this for me."

"Good for you. I have to work with him, so think about how awkward that is for me that he's sleeping with my sister," Taylor whispered.

"Damn right he is, and let me just say ... you missed out." Lucy winked sarcastically.

"That's gross, Lucy. Anyway, who else is here?"

"Jo and Eldon are, of course. You know anything to do with the arts they're going to be front and center. Oh, did she tell you?"

"Tell me what?" Taylor steeled herself. Family news could be earth shattering in their clan.

"Eldon is moving into the cabin with her and Levi in November." Lucy looked triumphant that she got to pass it on. "Soon as his lease is up on his apartment. Tomorrow, he's going back to New York to tie up some loose ends, then he's here permanently."

Taylor was surprised. "Wow. Jo has never let a man live with her because of Levi. This must really be serious. I wish she talked to us more about private things, so we could've seen it coming. Feels a bit fast for her."

She was a bit hurt that Jo hadn't talked to her about it first. Her sisters used to come to her for all big decisions.

"I saw it coming," Lucy said. "You're just never around. If you'd stop playing cops and robbers more often, you'd know more about what's happening at home, under your nose."

Before Taylor could defend herself, Faire joined them, looking elegant with her hair pulled into a soft chignon, bright green pieces of jade dangling from her ears to go with the colorful shawl she wore. Reading glasses propped on her head.

The entire combination made her look every bit the official

artist she was. The artist that now the whole town would refer to her as.

She nodded in agreement. "I'm so thankful to you for making this happen, Lucy. I feel like a star. Like a real artist."

Lucy's expression softened with gratitude. "You are both of those things, Faire. I couldn't have done it without your incredible art."

Faire leaned in. "We already have a very generous donation from some Atlanta folks who have a house here on the lake. They want to be benefactors of getting the new art center going."

"That's fantastic," Lucy said, her eyes lighting up with joy. "As long as I don't have to engrave their name on my forehead as acknowledgement. Now, go, make some more best friends, Faire. Let's make this a monumental art show for Hart's Ridge."

"It might be the only art show Hart's Ridge has had," Taylor said, questioning.

They laughed and Faire moved on, intent to talk to every person who came.

"Sam is here and he's looking sharp," Lucy said. "He left Alice with Cate. Every woman in here is eyeing him like he's a three-tier chocolate cake on the dessert buffet. You'd better attach yourself to him before someone devours him."

"Oh, God, I wish I would've had time to dress." Taylor looked down at her uniform and wished it was cut to at least fit her better, instead of making her look like a box.

"Don't worry about it. We'll just say you are security," Lucy said. "Try to look scary. Makes us even more official. On that note, Gotta go. I see someone waving at me. Hope it's a sale."

Taylor continued to explore the exhibition, moving through the crowd. She eventually found herself in front of the painting that had caught her eye during her earlier visit to Faire's house.

The painting portrayed Amos and David, a father and son who had tragically passed away together, extending their hands toward the wife and mother they had left behind. The artwork resonated with tangible emotions—the yearning, the affection, and the earnest desire to bridge the chasm between life and death. In the backdrop, a row of trees stood in neat alignment, while, beside the woman, a petite birch tree was adorned with a multitude of miniature, red sparrow ornaments.

Taylor's eyes welled up with tears as she gazed at the painting. It hurt to remember the scene she'd driven up to on the farm, but that was what instantly filled her mind. She wished she'd been a half hour earlier that day. The question never left her. Could she have saved them?

A paisley handkerchief appeared in front of her face, and she looked up to see the hand holding it belonged to Sam.

"Hi," she said, taking the cloth and dabbing her eyes.

He was wearing dress jeans with a white button-up shirt, a rustic but neat brown corduroy jacket over it. His boots shined like new money. She couldn't wait to be alone with him the whole next day on their road trip.

"You look great," she said through her sniffles.

"Thanks. Good timing, yeah?" he said, putting his arm around her. "What's the tears all about?"

She blew her nose and wiped her eyes, pulling herself together. "This piece represents a horrific tragedy we had in town before you got here. The Higgins own the Christmas tree farm out on the outskirts of town. Amos, the patriarch, and his son David were gunned down, along with David's best friend. Botched robbery."

Sam winced. "Ouch. Any survivors?"

Taylor looked around and saw Beverly coming at them.

"Yep. Incoming. His widow." She put a smile on her face. "Hi, Beverly. So good to see you."

"Taylor. Same. How have you been? I heard you got engaged." She looked pointedly at Taylor's hand, then at Sam.

"News travels fast," Taylor said, chuckling. "Here's the man himself. Sam, this is Beverly Higgins."

Sam gently shook her hand.

"This is quite an event, isn't it? Who would've thought what Faire was doing in this big ol' house by herself for so many years? A very nice little sur—" she turned slightly, noticing the painting behind Taylor, and she froze mid-sentence.

Taylor met Sam's eyes over her head, and he quietly walked away, leaving them alone.

"I take it this is your first time seeing it?" Taylor asked, putting her arm around Beverly, whose shoulders trembled as she cried.

"He really is with me," Beverly said, her words barely audible under her breath. "I was afraid he wasn't. That he was gone forever."

"Of course he's with you," Taylor said sympathetically. "He's all around you. David is, too. And Doug. They're all with you."

Her eldest son, Doug, had died in a motorcycle crash years before her son David had been slaughtered with his dad. She'd seen too much heartache in her life.

Beverly turned to her, her eyes wide and anxious. "No. Listen, Taylor. This is surreal that Faire captured this scene specifically. No one knows this, but I have a small garden that I've created in memory of Amos and David. I have the rocking chair out there that Amos made me, and I go there every morning. I planted a small birch tree right after he died, and it's only got one ornament. A red sparrow. From the very first Christmas we had as a family of five."

"That's so wonderful that she caught that for you," Taylor said.

Faire saw them in front of the painting and came over.

"Faire, how did you know?" Beverly asked softly, her eyes back on the painting.

"Because David told me," she said. "Did you know … birch trees represent new beginnings? Often thought of as a pioneer, the birch takes root in landscapes where no other tree would before."

Beverly's eyes filled with tears as she absorbed Faire's words.

"I ... I didn't know that. Amos was the tree guy. I just followed his lead, but I was drawn to that tree at a nursery in Ellijay, and I bought it not really knowing why. Then I decided it needed to be in a private garden for David. A place we can be together, and I can just talk to him."

She turned to Faire and took both her hands.

"I have to have it, Faire. Please tell me it's for sale. I don't care how much, I'll pay it," she said, pleadingly.

Faire reached out and gently touched Beverly's shoulder. "Of course. This painting, it's a gift to you, Beverly. To help you find closure with the tragedies that took your David and Amos from you too early."

Beverly was deeply moved, her voice quivering as she spoke. "Thank you, Faire. Thank you so much. I will treasure it until the day I die. Then Danny will keep it."

As Taylor watched the emotional exchange between the two women, she felt an overwhelming sense of pride for Faire and the incredible gift she possessed—the ability to capture not only the essence of the departed but also to offer solace and healing to those left behind. It was a beautiful and poignant moment, and she was suddenly glad she'd stopped in right when she did and had gotten to be a part of it.

CHAPTER 22

Taylor's footsteps echoed through Kathie Huff's small living room, the ticking clock on the wall serving as a relentless reminder of the time that had passed since she and Shane had closed the Swanson case. A week of solitude had been granted by the sheriff, a respite to heal and pursue her own case: unearthing the truth behind her traumatic past.

Sam and Kathie remained engrossed in their laptops, heads bowed low, their concentration unwavering. Taylor's emotions were inextricably entwined with the mystery she sought to unravel, and the weight of it clouded her thoughts.

Again, this morning, they had pieced together fragments of information: her attacker was the offspring of a woman named Blanche and had been adopted by a family in Hart County. Beyond those meager details, they had hit a brick wall.

Taylor paused at the window, her gaze drawn to Alice, who stood by the farm fence. Her gentle hand caressed one of the horses, while Kaiser, Kathie's dog, snuffled around her feet, following an invisible trail known only to him. The animals seemed to sense something in Alice, a quiet, serene spirit that attracted their trust.

The past week had seen Derek's abrupt appearance, bearing the grim news of Alice's mother's demise and his request that Alice come home to take care of her younger siblings. Normally, Taylor wouldn't see anything wrong with that, but there was something strange about the relationship between Alice and her dad. She said she'd rather drown herself than go back there without her mother as a buffer between them.

Sam had acted swiftly, enlisting the aid of a family law attorney. The results of a pending DNA test hung like a sword of Damocles, an uncertain fate that gnawed at their hearts. Sam, especially, was caught in a torment of fear—fear that the test would confirm Alice's connection to him, and fear that it wouldn't.

Alice's grief for her mother remained mostly unexpressed, having never culminated in a proper funeral. Derek had deemed it an extravagance for such a meager gathering, and, instead, Alice's mother had been cremated with only a small, somber family assembly.

Sam had escorted Alice, but he said it wasn't like any memorial he'd ever been to, and that it should've been more about Brooke than the dramafest it turned out to be.

Taylor had implored Sam to ask Derek to save a portion of the ashes for Alice, even offering to bear the cost of cremation. Sam, however, had insisted on handling the expenses, ensuring that Alice possessed a tangible link to her mother in the form of a necklace, a sacred vessel for a fragment of her ashes. Taylor had ordered three identical necklaces, ensuring that all the children would have the option to carry a piece of their mother with them.

Kathie finally glanced up from her laptop, her weariness etched across her features. She was doing a lot and only asking for a little. Sam had already done the work on her tractor, and had asked for more tasks to repay her, but she'd refused.

Taylor sank into a chair at the table, her frustration escalating.

"Taylor," Kathie confessed with a sigh, "I hate to say this, but I've hit a wall. I've reached out to every adoption agency in Mercer County and Hart. We'll need a warrant if we want to make any progress."

Taylor leaned forward, her mind racing for new avenues to explore. She really didn't want to bring in the sheriff just yet. If she did, he'd bring in Shane, and probably others.

"What about social media, using parameters based on possible birthdates? Birth announcements?"

Sam interjected, "Social media as we know it didn't exist back then."

"We've combed through newspaper birth announcements," Kathie added, her brow furrowing, "and found nothing. Online adoption registries have been scrutinized as well, but no one matching his details has applied to be matched."

Taylor sighed, the frustration and desperation of their search weighing heavily on her. "I appreciate everything you're both doing," she said, her gratitude tinged with helplessness.

Sam and Kathie had poured their hearts into the investigation, yet the pieces of the puzzle remained scattered. Taylor felt lost, uncertain of their next step.

They couldn't even consider the audacious idea of testing the DNA of men in the county. Not only would it be a likely insurmountable challenge, but the suspect may have long since moved away.

Kathie's voice softened with empathy as she reached out to console Taylor, offering understanding and support. In her presence, Taylor found a wellspring of strength.

Sam, equally disheartened by their lack of progress, voiced their only option. "We need to go back to Blanche."

Taylor recoiled at the thought. "You know she probably won't talk."

"It's our only option," Sam insisted. "We can drop Alice off at the farm with the kids and head straight to Bramwell. Kathie has her address, and we'll simply knock on her door."

"And then what?" Taylor retorted, her frustration bubbling over. "Hey, the son you relinquished to adoption grew up and attacked me. Now, we need his name so he can face justice?"

The words hung heavily in the air, leaving a bitter aftertaste. Taylor turned to Kathie, her eyes filled with a mixture of embarrassment and desperation.

Kathie approached and enveloped Taylor in a gentle embrace. "It's okay, Taylor," she whispered, her voice a soothing balm. "I already figured out why we were looking for him. Please don't feel ashamed. Let's just get this monster."

Her warmth and quiet strength steeled Taylor's resolve. She looked up at Sam, determination gleaming in her eyes.

"I'm ready," Taylor declared resolutely. "We'll make Blanche talk."

IT WAS after five o'clock when Sam brought his jeep to a stop in front of the Wagner residence. The stately house was nestled within a picturesque Bramwell neighborhood. Lush, manicured lawns stretched out before them, adorned with vibrant flowerbeds in full bloom. Towering oak trees offered a protective embrace to the elegant home, their leaves rustling gently in the breeze.

The lawn and the house were well kept with a look of attention that only came with professional (and expensive) preciseness.

"Ready?" Sam asked.

She nodded and they got out and walked up to the porch.

Taylor pressed the doorbell, their purpose today charging the atmosphere with an undeniable tension. Moments later, the grand double doors creaked open, revealing a small, dark-haired woman whose eyes widened in surprise.

Judging by the dust cloth and spray polisher she held, it was the housekeeper.

Taylor offered a warm smile and introduced themselves, "Hi, I'm Georgia Grayson, and this is my fiancé, Sam. We're here to see Mrs. Wagner. Is she available?"

The housekeeper hesitated for a moment, then nodded and stepped aside, welcoming them into the world of Blanche Wagner. The polished marble floors beneath their feet whispered a history of opulence and refinement.

Blanche Wagner emerged in the grand hallway, resplendent in an elegant, yet casual, outfit that perfectly harmonized with the upscale ambiance of her home. Her face lit up with a warm smile when she recognized Taylor and Sam. "Well, hello there! What a pleasant surprise. I thought you might be coming for a follow-up on that piece about Bramwell's history, but I didn't think you'd pop in unannounced, and at the dinner hour, too."

It was a passive-aggressive statement, but Taylor maintained a friendly demeanor, though her heart raced with the knowledge of the bombshell it carried. "Actually, Mrs. Wagner, we're here for a different reason today. May we have a moment of your time?"

Blanche's expression shifted; her curiosity now tinged with apprehension. "Of course, dear. Please, come into the sitting room. What's this about?"

The trio moved through the grand house, passing exquisite tapestries and antique furniture that spoke of wealth and taste. They finally reached a big sunroom with large windows that—if it was earlier in the day—would surely flood the space with natural light. Lamps were lit and the room was adorned with potted plants and comfortable furnishings, creating an inviting atmosphere.

Blanche gestured for them to sit on the white sofa.

Taylor leaned forward; her voice measured. "Mrs. Wagner, before we get to why we're here, we'd like to hear more of your story. Could you tell us about how you met Henry and the life you built together?"

"Will this be part of the story you're doing?" she asked, looking curious.

"Possibly," Taylor said.

Blanche's eyes clouded with a mix of nostalgia and sadness as she recalled the past. "Oh, Henry and I met at a charity gala. I was working there as a volunteer, and he was one of the guests. I couldn't believe my luck when he approached me. Someone from a family as prestigious as the Wagners being interested in me ... it was like a dream come true. What else do you want to know?"

When she stopped, Taylor knew it was time to come clean. She pulled out her badge and showed it and Blanche's eyes widened in shock.

"Mrs. Wagner, I'm sorry, but my name is not Georgia Grayson. It's Taylor Gray, and I'm a sheriff's deputy for Hart County, Georgia. I've been talking to you because of an investigation we are doing into something that involves one of your sons."

Blanche's face went white.

"What do you mean? Which son? My boys aren't criminals."

"The boys that you know and raised may not be, but, I promise you, your first son might be involved in a serious crime."

"My first son?" she hedged.

Taylor nodded. "Yes, your first son. The one who you relinquished to adoption."

Blanche was quiet for another moment. "How did you find out? The records are sealed."

"Like I said, I'm in law enforcement and we have ways of learning things that the average citizen doesn't. I can assure you that no one other than us and my superior know your connection to him."

"Tell me what he has done," Blanche said. Gone was all the hospitality and smiles, and she suddenly looked older by many years.

"Allegedly done. But first, please go on with your story about meeting Henry," Taylor said. "As long as it will lead to the son."

Blanche looked from Taylor to Sam, then back to Taylor. She took a deep breath, then continued, her voice wavering slightly as the memories flooded back. "Everything was perfect between us, except for one thing. You see, I was already pregnant with the child of a man who had no means and an even meaner temper. I didn't want to give my child away, but I knew it was my only chance at me having a different kind of life than my mother had lived, than anyone in my family had lived. I could be someone, with Henry beside me, and his name as mine."

"Go on," Sam said gently.

Tears welled up in Blanche's eyes, but she pressed on with her story. "So, I made the hardest decision of my life. I relinquished my child to adoption, and, along with that, I gave up everything about my current life to be with Henry. But I never forgot about that baby." She wiped away a tear and continued, her voice tinged with regret. "I've carried that secret with me all these years, the pain of giving up my own flesh and blood. It was the price I had to pay to be with Henry, to live this life of privilege and status."

Sam spoke gently. "Mrs. Wagner, we understand that this is difficult for you. We're here to uncover the truth, but we'll do our best to protect your name and reputation. Can you please tell us about the family who adopted your child? Their name, any information you have."

Blanche hesitated, "I swear, I don't know their name," she finally admitted, her voice barely above a whisper. "They were kind people, and they promised to provide a good life for my baby, but the terms were that I would not know their name. Once a year they would send photos to a post office box number that I set up, and that would be my only connection. They did that.

Eighteen photos, one for each year, but I never tried to track them down. I let my son have his life, and I had mine."

"Do you have any of the photos here?" Taylor asked.

Blanche hesitated.

"If what you say is true," Taylor added. "Then you kept those photos."

"I'll be right back," Blanche said, then rose and left the room.

"What do you think?" Sam said, when she was gone. "Do you think she knows their name and isn't telling?"

"If she does, she's a great liar. Hopefully we'll find a clue in the photos."

Blanche returned and handed Taylor a thick manila envelope. "I closed out the post office box after Henry died. I keep the photos here with me now. In a place my sons can't stumble upon."

Taylor opened the envelope and slid the stack of photos out into her hands.

"I've left them in order," Blanche said.

She had, and the first photo was of a chubby infant, one year of age. He sat in a crib, gazing up at the camera, a partial smile on his face.

Taylor wouldn't say he looked happy, especially. Maybe curious was the more appropriate term.

Sam came to look over her shoulder and Taylor flipped through the photos, all an impeccably dressed, if not overly posed, child, before stopping at the one for year twelve.

In this photo, he was starting to grow out of his boyish looks. His face was less chubby and developing more mature angles. He looked familiar.

She studied his face, trying to figure out why, but then went to the next photo. He was thirteen.

Same feeling.

She'd seen that kid somewhere.

When she got to year fifteen, she stopped and felt tingles leave her fingers and travel up her arms. This time—in the boy's face—she could see the man he would become. She felt waves of disbelief before they were replaced with nausea.

For so many years she'd imagined her attacker as a total stranger. Someone who had picked her at random. Someone she'd never laid eyes on before the incident, or after. Now to see that it was someone she knew and trusted, someone who looked into her eyes and spoke to her frequently, like he'd done nothing wrong, disgusted her and made her feel so much dirtier than he'd made her feel before.

"Taylor, what's wrong?" Sam said, putting his hand on her shoulder. "Are you okay?"

She threw the photos down on the side table and ran out the door, barely making it to the fancy, manicured shrubs before she lost the contents of her stomach.

Sam came outside and held her hair back for the final retches, then guided her to the steps and helped her sit down before going inside to bring her back a wet paper towel. It was getting late, and the moonlight cast an eerie glow on the front lawn, adding to the surreal and haunting moment.

"I recognized him, too," he said. "He's a rotten, depraved piece of shit. I can't wait to get my hands on him. What do we do now? Go to the sheriff?"

He'd told Blanche to stay inside, and Taylor was relieved she wouldn't have to face her again. She felt like everyone could see her story on her face. She felt exposed and assaulted all over again. What she wanted was a marathon scalding shower, but first she had to get back to the farm. Her family was in danger, and they didn't even know it.

"Yes, but first we need to get to the farm. I'm worried about my sisters."

When she felt her legs would carry her safely again, Sam

helped her to the jeep. As they left the stately house, they carried Blanche's story and the identity of her attacker with them, a reminder that secrets ran deep, and the past had a way of resurfacing when least expected.

CHAPTER 23

*T*he urgency to get home weighed heavy on Taylor's chest as she and Sam sped down the highway, breaking every traffic law in sight. They barely talked, both lost in their own thoughts and fears.

They covered the distance at breakneck speed, making record time. The usually scenic drive passed in a blur of green and brown, Taylor's mind consumed with worry.

Upon arrival, the farm seemed eerily silent. Without pausing, Taylor dashed straight to Jo's cabin. No answer. The ominous feeling deepened. They rushed to Anna's house, calling out, pounding on the door. Silence responded.

Panic gripped Taylor; she checked her watch, realizing it was past the kids' bedtime. Everyone should be home, tucked safely behind locked doors.

She fumbled with her phone, dialing Cate first. Rings echoed in her ear before going to voicemail. Then she tried her sisters. No answer. With a sinking feeling, she dialed her father. The familiar gruff voice answered, but concern immediately tinted it as she hastily asked about the others.

"Taylor, I haven't seen anyone. What's wrong? What's going on?" Her dad's voice resonated with a rising panic.

She hesitated, then simply said, "I can't explain right now." Without another word, she hung up.

She turned to Sam, her voice trembling. "We need to search the property. They must be here." But first, she needed her gun. They headed to her cabin where she quickly retrieved her weapon. She noted Diesel, her dog, pacing nervously, his eyes darting, sensing the tension. Sam reassuringly patted his holster, confirming he was armed as well.

They left Diesel inside for his own safety, despite his attempts to stay with them, and Taylor led the way to the small barn, signaling for Sam to stay back. Though he hesitated, he understood the importance of the divide and conquer strategy in this situation. Inside, the barn seemed untouched; Apollo nickered softly in his stall while the goats stirred at the far end. Relieved that the barn was clear, she returned outside and nodded to Sam.

Their next destination was the largest building on the property, the dog-boarding facility. The weight of uncertainty and fear gnawed at Taylor with each step she took. She slowly opened the door, straining her ears for any sound. None of the dogs were barking, but they wouldn't at this time of night, unless they heard something unusual.

Suddenly, a cold, metallic sensation pressed against her temple. The door slammed shut behind her, and, among the chorus of a dozen dogs barking as hard as they could, a familiar voice sneered next to her ear, "Thought I was in New York, didn't you? You think Blanche wouldn't tip me off? I've been squeezing secrets out of that woman for years, Taylor. She'll do anything to protect her little world."

Eldon's voice dripped with venom. Taylor forced herself to remain calm, focusing on his words, looking for an opening, a hint about her family's whereabouts. She hoped Sam had the sense to stay hidden and call for backup.

"Why me, Eldon?" she managed, her voice steady.

His eyes bore into hers, gleaming with malice. "Two reasons, Taylor. It should've been Anna, but she was locked up tight in her fancy neighborhood, a husband, and them clingy-assed kids always around."

The dogs calmed when they saw it was her, a relief in the already tense moment of Taylor trying to figure out what to do next.

She was completely baffled. "Anna? Why Anna? What has she ever done to you?"

He pushed her forward angrily. "Don't act like you don't know what she did to me. She thought she was better than everyone at school. The bleach blonde cheerleader. Dating the most popular boys. All it took was one joke from her about me and my high school life was ruined."

"I'm not following," Taylor tells him. "I thought you loved high school. You and Jo were such good friends. You got just about every lead in the drama productions. Both of you did."

"Oh, yeah. I loved high school," he says sarcastically. "I loved that instantly, after Anna's endorsement, I was labeled a drama queen queer. In one statement, Anna stripped away every bit of masculinity that I had in that one statement. Yeah, that was great, Taylor. You know what else was great? Not one other girl in the school would talk to me after that. Only Jo."

"Eldon, listen to yourself. It was high school. Everyone has a tough time in high school. You think it was fun for me? I had to keep three sisters on the straight and narrow. Make sure they did their homework. Were fed. Stayed out of trouble. I was working a full-time, minimum waged job, going to high school, and taking care of a family back then. And you're worried about a little rumor?"

"It wasn't a little rumor," he spat out. "It followed me everywhere. It took my dignity. I had no respect. I had to move to New York City to escape it. Everyone in town has always looked at me like I have the plague. You think I wanted to constantly defend myself?"

"I think that it shouldn't matter what other people think," she said, intent to keep him talking. "My dad was a drunk and, because of him, we were dirt poor and bounced in and out of foster care. Don't you think that follows me everywhere I go?"

He looked at her with dead eyes. So cold. So different than she'd ever thought he could be. "So, you don't love Jo? This whole thing was a vendetta to get back at us?"

"I didn't love her back then," he says, and she hears something in his voice that makes her think maybe she can get out of her predicament. "She's nothing like the rest of you. She isn't a redneck, country bumpkin, and she should've left Hart's Ridge a long time ago to get her son out of these sticks."

So, Jo was his weak spot. Taylor would use it. "She loves you, Eldon. And Levi does, too. What about him?"

"Leave him out of this," he screamed.

She tried to backtrack to calm him again. "You said you came after me for two reasons. What was the other one?"

His voice was deadly again. Less emotional and more matter of fact. "Simple. You stole this place from me. I used to come by all the time, you know. Sit out on the dock when you were asleep. Enjoy what should've been mine."

"I swear, Eldon, I have no idea what you are talking about." Taylor is completely confused. "This place? The farm? What do you mean? It belonged to my father before me."

"And it belonged to my family before him. My adoptive family, that is. How ironic is it that it was sold out from under my dad for back taxes, and we had to live in a trailer even as I watched all of you get off the bus at my house every day. How do you think that made me feel?"

"We didn't know that, Eldon," Taylor cried. "We were kids! When we moved here, it was for sale and that's all we knew. Did you ever tell Jo?"

He laughed bitterly. "Why would I? Then of all the irony, your dad lost it for the same reason my dad did. This was going to be my own sanctuary one day. Somewhere away from the eyes and judgment of everyone who once made my life hell. But I was left with nothing."

"Then my dad is the one to be angry at, not me."

"You're missing the point," he screamed. "This place was going to be the only damn thing I ever got from anyone. With what you've made it into, your family will never leave it. My dad is still living in our tiny trailer, drinking himself to death."

"Sounds familiar." Taylor thought of her own dad's dismal trailer. Then she wondered desperately where Sam was. "So, what's your plan, Eldon? You think that getting rid of me will set everything right?"

He narrowed his eyes at her. "Don't talk to me like I'm stupid. And don't try the psychobabble talk either. I've had years of that crap and I'm immune to it. I prefer to exorcise my demons on stage, when I can be anyone I want to be. Anyone but who I really am." He pushed her forward, toward the meeting room where the door is closed.

"Surely you're more articulate than that. Tell me what I did wrong. Not my father, but me. Why would you do to me what you did?"

"Remember the rose on your car?"

Of course she did. She'd thought that Shane had left it.

"I had fun toying with you, Taylor," he sneered. "I've watched you all these years when I came to town. You and Anna. But you were the easy target that night. A replacement for what I wanted to do to get back at Anna. But it's deeper than that. It's about the farm, about reclaiming what's mine. You took it, and now you've turned it into some sort of family and animal haven."

Taylor felt a mix of anger and disbelief. "So, you assaulted me because of high school and land? This is madness, Eldon."

His grip on the gun tightened. "It's not madness at all. It's

199

about respect, about belonging. Your family took everything from me since the time I was fifteen years old, and now I want to take everything from you."

Time seemed to stretch and warp as Eldon continued his tirade, and it had only been about six or seven minutes, but every second that passed was another second closer to rescue. She just needed to keep him talking, to keep his attention on her and away from her family.

As he shoved her forward toward the closed door of their meeting room, all Taylor could do was pray everyone else was safe and that help was on its way.

Her breath hitched as Eldon thrust the door open, revealing her family. They were huddled together behind the overturned table, seeking refuge from the looming threat. Anna shielded her children with a mother's fierce, protective instinct. Levi was beside Jo, who cradled a blessedly sleeping Johnny. Alice was on the other side of her, clinging to her arm.

But Lucy, in her usual bravado, sat confidently, glaring daggers at Eldon.

"I always knew you were a little sissy," Lucy spat, an edge to her voice. "Have to have a gun to make you feel like a man, don't you? Does the feel of it in your hands make up for your shriveled, little penis?"

Eldon's eyes flashed with rage, his grip on the gun tightening. He shoved Taylor forward, causing her to stumble into Lucy. Johnny's wails echoed in the room, creating an atmosphere of piercing anxiety.

"Lucy! Now's not the time!" Taylor hissed, her fear clear. But she couldn't help but secretly admire Lucy's unyielding spirit.

Jo, tears streaking her face, tried reasoning with Eldon, "Tell me what is going on, Eldon. Please. You're ruining everything. What about the life we're building together? Our theater camp dream?"

His eyes darted toward her; twisted anguish evident. "Too late for all that, Jo. All because Taylor here couldn't let sleeping dogs lie. Had to go around playing Nancy Drew, sticking her nose where it doesn't belong and digging up my past."

"Then maybe you shouldn't have broken into my house four years ago to rape me!" Taylor shot back, her voice quivering with rage and heartache.

The room went silent, the weight of her revelation palpable.

Jo seemed at a loss for words. She was shaking her head in denial, even as she spoke. "Wait. What did you say, Taylor?"

This wasn't how she wanted it to come out and Taylor wished she could put the words back in her mouth and choke them back. "I'm sorry, Jo. It's true. Eldon assaulted me several years ago. I have irrefutable evidence. It was him but it took me this long to figure it out."

Jo looked at Eldon, her voice broke as she spoke. "I thought you came back to this town to find me. That's what you said. You said you couldn't stop thinking about me and that now you want us to be a family. You, me, and Levi. We're going to open our own theatre camp. We made dreams together, Eldon. I trusted you. What have you done?"

Her words were heavy with sadness and disbelief.

Suddenly, Levi, in a surge of youthful bravery and fury, broke away from the group and lunged at Eldon, fists flying, tears pouring. "You lied! You lied!" he screamed, voice raw with betrayal.

As Eldon flailed with the gun, trying to fend off Levi, Taylor saw her chance. "Run!" she screamed, leaping at Eldon. Levi scrambled out of the way as they tumbled to the ground, the gun skittering away. In the chaos, everyone but Cate bolted from the room.

Cate, desperate to help Taylor, tried to wrestle Eldon off her.

"Get the gun, Cate!" Taylor screamed.

Suddenly, Sam appeared, eyes blazing. "Let her go!" he roared, hauling Eldon off Taylor, and shoving him to the side, but, unfortunately, directly toward the gun that lay within reach.

Taylor scrambled to her feet, her heart pounding, lungs gasping for air.

But Eldon, eyes crazed and bloodied lip dripping, wasn't finished. He lunged for his gun at the same time as Cate.

He was closer. Just as he grabbed it, Sam drew his own, and the two faced off in a tense standoff.

"Don't try it," Sam warned. His hands were shaking badly. He wasn't used to handling weapons.

Alice was wild-eyed, begging Eldon not to shoot Sam.

"Calm down, everyone," Taylor said, her voice even and authoritative. "Eldon, right now we can work things out. But if you pull that trigger, and someone dies, you'll never see the light of day again."

"Shut the hell up, Taylor!" Eldon screamed, the cords in his neck bulging. "You're the reason this is happening, you stupid bitch. You just had to go snooping around. Pulling information out of Blanche. You should've let it go!"

Seeing the barrel of his gun pointed directly at the love of her life sent a shiver of terror through her like she'd never known. She prayed silently. Surely God wouldn't take him from her. Not like this, not when she'd dragged him into something that had nothing to do with him.

A voice then bellowed from the doorway. "Hello, Eldon."

It was Jackson, Taylor's father, gun pointed and face grim.

Eldon whipped around and pointed the gun at him.

"No one threatens my family. Goodbye, Eldon," Jackson said.

Taylor screamed, but it was Cate's voice, filled with terror, that pierced the standoff the most and, with it, her mother jumped between the two groups, her back to Jackson in a protective stance.

"No, don't shoot. If everyone would just calm down and hold their—" she began to say.

Her plea was interrupted by two gunshots that cracked

through the air simultaneously, their reverberations echoing in the sudden silence that followed.

Jo screamed out in anguish as Eldon crumpled to the floor.

Taylor wasn't sad to see it happen.

But there was collateral damage.

Horrified, her world instantly crumbled. Cate, with a rapidly growing red stain on her blouse, had also fallen. She grabbed her chest, and her expression was one of wide-eyed disbelief.

Jackson screamed, a deep guttural sound that sounded like a wild animal.

"No! Oh my God, Mom!" Taylor yelled, collapsing beside her mother as the weight of the moment bore down on her, dragging her into a vortex of despair. For many years, she'd thought she didn't have a mother. Now that she did, and Cate was such an important part of her life, of everyone's life, she couldn't imagine not having her.

She gathered Cate into her arms and rocked back and forth with her, begging her to stay awake. Fate had once again turned and trampled all over the Gray family.

CHAPTER 24

The siren wailed loudly as the ambulance sped down the streets, tearing through the cool night. Inside, a flurry of activity unfolded. Cate lay on the stretcher, an oxygen mask pressed over her face, while the paramedic, John, worked quickly to stem the blood flow from the gunshot wound to her chest. The blood-soaked bandage was replaced every few minutes, the crimson liquid threatening to overpower it each time.

Jackson had wanted to be in the ambulance with Cate, but the paramedics had said they only had space for one family member.

Taylor wasn't about to give up that spot.

She held Cate's hand tightly. "Stay with me, Mom. Please," she whispered, her eyes glistening with tears. "Don't leave me."

Cate didn't answer.

She hadn't realized that she'd called Cate *Mom* until the third or fourth time she heard it come out of her mouth. It felt so right and natural that she'd never call her anything else again. With that realization, she also understood that she'd forgiven Cate for leaving her so long ago. For putting her in the position of caring for her sisters, and for the years of longing for a mother and only having an irresponsible father to barely depend on.

John, the paramedic, worked diligently, his movements swift and sure. "Pressure dressing is in place," he murmured to his partner. "Pulse is thready, but she's hanging on."

Every bump on the road was a jolt to Taylor's heart, her gaze never leaving her mother's pale face. Cate's eyelids flickered, showing glimpses of the pain she was in.

She never spoke, and that was terrifying.

"It's okay, Mom. We're almost there," Taylor said, brushing a strand of hair off Cate's forehead. "You're going to be fine."

She didn't know if that was the truth or not.

The ambulance screeched to a halt outside the hospital's emergency entrance. Instantly, a team of doctors and nurses were on hand, wheeling Cate straight into the surgery wing. The white lights overhead blurred as they rushed her down the hallways, leaving Taylor trailing behind, feeling helpless.

When they got to a set of double doors that said "Medical Personnel Only," a nurse told her to go to the waiting room.

Taylor turned, and, like a zombie, went from one waiting room to the other, finally finding her family. Teague and Bronwyn sat in chairs on either side of Anna, who kept her arms around them and had them pulled close, like a mother bird over her chicks. Jackson paced the floor, his shoes making a rhythmic sound on the tiles.

Jo sat with Levi, rubbing his back as she talked softly to him. He had tears running down his face, a sight that made Taylor angry and sad all at once.

All the kids were going to need some intense therapy from the trauma they'd been involved in. She suddenly wished she'd been the one to kill Eldon. The anger she felt rise in her was like something she'd never felt.

Her family was everything to her and she'd failed them. After everything she'd learned in her career, when they needed her, she'd not been there. She should've been smarter—or faster.

Then she would've figured things out sooner and avoided the blood bath.

If her mom died because of her ...

Lucy was the first to rush to her, and she held her arms out. Taylor nearly fell into them, suddenly weak on her feet. Jackson saw her falter and took her from Lucy, guiding her to a chair.

"How is she?" they asked together, as though one voice.

Everyone froze, waiting on her to answer.

"She's still alive," Taylor said, her voice hoarse with emotion. "They took her to surgery."

"Will she be okay?" Jackson asked desperately.

Taylor turned to look at him. "I don't know, Dad. It depends on how close the gunshot is to her heart. It's a good sign that she wasn't killed instantly, but the bullet could've chipped a major blood vessel. She's in a lot of trouble."

No one said anything, and the fear and sorrow were so thick it was hard to breathe.

"Where's Sam?" Taylor asked, suddenly realizing he wasn't there. She didn't see Alice either. Where had they gone?

Her breath caught in her throat.

"I'm right here."

Sam came walking through the doorway, Alice on his heels. He had a tray loaded down with cups and donuts.

"How's Cate?" he asked, setting the tray on one of the side tables.

Alice began passing the cups to the younger kids, then handing each of them a donut. She'd stepped into her regular role, even though it wasn't her siblings she was caring for.

"She's in surgery," Taylor said.

When she looked at him, she couldn't keep the fear out of her eyes.

Sam came to her and pulled her out of her chair and into his arms, and the floodgates were opened. Uncharacteristically for her, she broke into ragged sobs as she clung to him.

"It'll be okay," he whispered to her.

"What—what if it's not?" she choked out.

He stroked her hair. "It will, Taylor. Believe it. Don't think of the alternative."

Finally, she calmed herself, embarrassed that she'd lost her composure in front of everyone, especially the kids. They were used to seeing Aunt Taylor as strong, dependable, and the one who was usually the steady one amid the storms.

"Come on," Sam said, leading her to a chair. "Drink some coffee. Or do you want hot chocolate? A donut, maybe?"

"Just coffee, please." Quickly she texted the sheriff to ask when he'd be there. She'd already called the team to the scene, and lights had pulled up to the farm just as the ambulance pulled out. Lucy said she'd fill Shane in on the details, but Taylor needed to tell the sheriff everything that Lucy didn't know. It could be a while before he came, as he'd want to secure the crime scene himself before coming to get their statements, but she also wanted him there just to confirm that Eldon was dead.

The sheriff would expect her to still be professional. She tried to catalog everything in her mind, to organize it, but she kept seeing Cate's pale face in her mind. She thought of Ellis, and that she should call him.

Usually, she was great at making snap decisions, but she felt paralyzed now, unable to do anything until someone confirmed that Cate was going to be okay.

Sam sat down next to her and held her hand, and Taylor forgot Ellis and every other thing she should be doing. She thought of nothing but her mother.

And she prayed.

Stolen glances at her sisters showed they were doing it, too, between moments of taking care of the kids.

Cecil appeared around the corner and Taylor jumped to her feet, embracing him. His solid and dependable presence sent her into tears again.

"Taylor, I'm so sorry I wasn't there," he said against her hair. "I was spending the night at my house in town."

"No, I'm glad you weren't there." If something had happened to him, she would've lost her mind.

"Tell me everything," he said, breaking away and leading her to a chair.

His hands were so warm, and she clutched them as she began.

Quietly, so that the kids wouldn't have to relive the incident, she filled him in. Cecil was just as shocked as she was that Eldon had fooled them all. He had always come off as such a nice person, though now Taylor was remembering some moments that, in hindsight, could be questioned.

"He's a madman," Cecil said. "It's simply unbelievable."

"I'd love to get my hands on him," Jackson said, his anger making him sound older.

No one would be getting their hands on Eldon, other than the medical examiner and whoever dealt with preparing him for death.

Taylor saw Cecil peek at Jo, and pity replaced his anger.

Jo looked shell-shocked and Taylor couldn't imagine the guilt she was feeling, probably thinking that she was responsible for everything. Taylor would have to make her see that it had nothing to do with her—it was all Taylor's fault.

Cecil didn't ask any more questions. It wasn't the right time or place. Everyone settled into silence again, only broken by the mindless chattering of women arguing with each other in some reality show that played on the television mounted in the corner of the room.

Hours seemed to stretch on endlessly. The sterile smell of the hospital, the soft whispers, the stifled sobs, and the noise of the television. Every now and then a code called on the intercom, or a rushing of feet scrambled down the hall to an emergency.

It all created an atmosphere of tension.

Another family joined them, shuffling in, settling on the other side of the waiting room, their expressions a mirror image of the grief and anxiety that Taylor's family bore. It was a family of five: an elderly couple, a younger woman, and two young children. The grandmother, with silver hair tied in a neat bun, clutched a rosary, the beads slipping through her fingers with every prayer. The grandfather's eyes were red-rimmed, his hand resting on the back of the young woman, who looked no older than Taylor as she tended to her children.

Taylor heard her call him dad. Her face was pale, her eyes constantly darting toward the hall, waiting for any news. Her children, a boy and a girl no older than Bronwyn, sat beside her, coloring books sprawled in front of them. But it was evident they were only trying to distract themselves, their crayon strokes aggressive in their buried unease.

"Car accident," the old woman finally whispered to Taylor, as though she'd asked. "My son was driving home from work when a truck hit him. They had to cut him from the car."

Taylor felt a pang of sympathy. She thought of the countless accident scenes she'd attended over the years. Scenes tense with overturned cars, the frantic calls over the radio, the cries of the injured and shocked. She remembered the faces of family members when they arrived, their expressions shifting rapidly between hope, fear, and uncertainty.

"I'm sorry," she said softly. "I'm a sheriff's deputy, and I've seen many families go through this. Just hold on to faith. It's the strongest thing you have right now."

The grandmother looked up, her eyes filled with gratitude. "Thank you," she said, clutching her rosary tighter as she turned her attention back to her grandchildren.

An hour later, all the kids in the room were getting tired and cranky. They'd found places to lean on to close their eyes, whether it was against the wall, or next to someone, snuggled into whatever softness they could find.

They should be home and tucked in bed, and Taylor felt anger surge again at the chaos that Eldon had caused. Suddenly she remembered that, despite the chaos, she'd forgotten that she'd finally solved her own case and would no longer have to look over her shoulder and wonder if her attacker was watching.

She wished now that he wasn't dead. That she could see him spend the rest of his life in a cage, behind bars and far from the drama of the stage that he so loved.

Stop thinking of him now, she told herself. *Focus on Cate.*

Taylor was taking her turn with Johnny, and she cradled him on her lap, though he was so tall now that his lower legs were across Sam. His head was heavy over one of her arms, but she didn't mind. It was a fair trade off because she was using the intoxicating little boy scent of him to try to calm her anxiety, breathing him in when her pulse raced off and on.

Lucy was like a lion in a cage, just like their dad. She took after him in so many ways and they both paced quietly, expressions of revenge across their face.

Everyone jumped when the doors finally swung open, revealing a tall man in blue scrubs, his face weary but composed.

"I'm Dr. Reynolds," he began. "Who here is the spokesperson for Catherine Gray?"

Without hesitation, Jackson stepped forward, "I am. I'm her husband."

Taylor rose from her seat, her voice clear but shaking. "No, Dr. Reynolds. They aren't married any longer. I'm her eldest daughter. I'll speak for my mother."

Jackson shot her an angry look, but this was no time to placate him as she usually did.

A brief moment of confusion crossed Dr. Reynolds' face, but he quickly moved on. "Can the adults please step out here in the hallway?'

Taylor led the way and Jackson, Jo, Lucy, and Anna followed. Sam stayed back with the kids.

The doctor looked gravely concerned. "Cate made it through surgery. The bullet missed her heart by mere centimeters. We managed to control the bleeding, and she's now in intensive care. The next twenty-four hours will be crucial."

"Will she make it?" Taylor asked.

"I can't make you any promises, but we are doing everything we can," he said, crossing his arms over his chest.

"So now what?" Jackson asked.

"If she pulls through, you can expect her to be on a ventilator for a few days, and then, once she's stable enough, we will start her on physical therapy."

That he was talking about physical therapy was encouraging, and Taylor felt a tiny shred of hopefulness. He smashed it in the next statement.

"Look, I don't want to mislead you," he said. "I want you to be optimistic but also you have to know this is going to a very hard night for her. However, despite the damage done to her body, she's made it this far and—make no mistake—that is a miracle. It tells me that your mother is a fighter."

"Damn straight she is," Lucy said, her jaw set tight.

Jackson nodded in agreement.

The doctor smiled sympathetically. "I also see from her burn scars that she's won a major health battle before. That bodes well for what she's up against because now it's all up to her and her inner strength. Looks like she's got plenty, so take hope in that, but, if you believe in a higher power, you need to be praying."

Taylor nodded, her eyes filled with gratitude. "We will. Thank you, Dr. Reynolds."

The surgeon placed a hand on Taylor's shoulder, his touch gentle. "It's a good thing she is a fighter, because she'll need every bit of fight she can muster to recover, and it will be a long journey. But let's take it one hour at a time."

He left them and they all huddled together.

One hour at a time would be excruciating.

The waiting game had begun, but they had hope, and Taylor had learned a long time ago that—sometimes—that's all you needed.

A<small>RE</small> you ready for more Hart's Ridge? You can get book eight, STARTING OVER, now at the following link:

DOWNLOAD *Starting Over*

Starting Over, the eighth book in the Hart's Ridge small-town mystery series by Kay Bratt, showcases the Gray family's unwavering strength as they face a crisis that threatens to tear them apart. When tragedy is on their doorstep and threatening to barge inside, they must come together to find the courage and hope to start anew.

Readers will be moved by the Gray family's resilience in the face of adversity, and heartened by the support they receive from the close-knit community of Hart's Ridge. But as they delve deeper into the story, they will realize that even the strongest bonds can be tested by secrets that have been kept hidden for far too long.

With Bratt's familiar emotional storytelling, *Starting Over* is a gripping tale of family and forgiveness that reminds us that tragedy can be a source of strength, and that hope is the key to overcoming even the darkest of times.

Starting Over is book eight of the new Hart's Ridge small-town mystery series, written by Kay Bratt, million-copy best-selling author of Wish Me Home and True to Me.

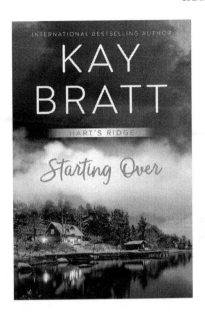

Get Starting Over [here]

Please join my monthly newsletter to learn more about me and the Bratt Pack, and to be notified of new releases, sales, and giveaways! JOIN KAY'S NEWSLETTER HERE

FROM THE AUTHOR

Hello, readers! I hope you enjoyed *Hello Goodbye*, the seventh book in the *Hart's Ridge* series. The true crime wrapped into the fictional town of Hart's Ridge and its fictional characters was loosely inspired by a double murder referred to in which Lawrence Swartz killed his adoptive parents, Bob and Kathryn "Kay" Swartz. As in my story, the eldest son, Michael, was the prime suspect because of his history with rebellion and his tumultuous relationship with his adoptive father. Lawrence "Larry" Swartz was the younger brother and considered somewhat of a golden boy who got good grades, made close friends, and strived for his parents' favor. He was the least likely suspect until the handprint came back from the FBI lab, and then he was charged with the murders. He claimed innocence all the way up to the day of his trial, in which he finally confessed. The judge was torn because of the severity of the crime and felt there were extenuating circumstances in how the parents disciplined their sons, pushing Larry to snap. He pled guilty and was released after only nine years behind bars.

Larry moved to Florida and married, then died at age 38 from a heart attack. In a twist of fate, his older brother Michael was later arrested at the age of 25 for a botched robbery that ended in murder. He was sentenced to life in prison without the possibility of parole, and a man lost his life, over the attempted theft of a measly jar of coins.

Their little sister, Anne Swartz, was adopted by family friends after a lengthy custody battle with Kathryn's sister. Anne went on to marry and have two children, one of them a son that she named Larry.

So, what's next? Well, I hope you are still staying with me for the next book, Starting Over. At book number eight, it was originally going to be the last. Now that we are this far, and the series has been such an amazing success, I'm rethinking stopping at eight books. There are still so many storylines in my head that could go anywhere, and as long as readers still want more of the Gray family, and they are showing me with sales and positive reviews, I'll try to keep it going. I know you all want to see if Taylor gets her happily ever after, right? And what about Cate? Will her new life with her family be cut short?

I think we should keep up with all the Gray women and hopefully at least a few of them will see some sort of resolution. Maybe all! Wouldn't that be great? Just remember. My stories are realistic, and I don't take the easy way. Just like my own life, my characters must traverse through ups and downs, and all arounds. What I hope is that following along with their trials and successes, we can all learn from the themes of hardship, resilience, and forgiveness that is woven through the pages (and fictional streets) of Hart's Ridge.

I'm blessed to be able to earn a living doing what I love, and that would not be possible without reader support, so thank you. An even bigger dose of gratitude to those in my private Facebook group, Kay's Krew, who are always there to support me when I'm having a bad day, writer's block, or just need to smile. I'm also known to entertain there with stories of my life with the Bratt Pack and all the kerfuffles I find myself getting into.

Want to skip the fluff and just know what I'm writing? You can join my author newsletter to hear of future Hart's Ridge books, as well as participate in giveaways and sales.

Until then,

Scatter kindness everywhere.

Kay Bratt

ABOUT THE AUTHOR

Kay Bratt learned to lean on writing while she navigated a tumultuous childhood and then a decade of domestic abuse in adulthood. After working her way through the hard years to come out a survivor and a pursuer of peace, she finally found the courage to use her experiences throughout her novels, most recently *Wish Me Home* and *True to Me*. Her books have fueled many exciting book club discussions and have made it into the hands of more than a million readers across the world. She lives with the love of her life and her rescue dogs on the banks of Lake Hartwell in Georgia, USA.

For more information, visit www.kaybratt.com.

Made in the USA
Columbia, SC
06 May 2024

35350212R00136